Where She Belongs

Laurel Ridge Series, Book #9

Tara Baisden

Sterling Ridge Press LLC

Cover designed by Sterling Ridge Press LLC

Published by: Sterling Ridge Press, LLC www.sterlingridgepress.com

ISBN: 978-1-966093-08-4 Printed in the United States of America

First Edition: April 2025

For permissions, contact: tara@tarabaisden.com or visit www.tarabaisden.com

Also by Tara Baisden

<u>Riverbend Valley Series</u>

#1 A Cowboy's Second Chance

#2 Wanderlust & Wild Horses

#3 Heartstrings on the Horizon

<u>Laurel Ridge Series</u>

#1. Season of Hope

#2. Finding Grace

#3. His Perfect Plan

#4. Love Redeemed

#5 Snowbound Blessings

#6 Sheltered Hearts

#7 Restoring Faith

#8 Love Rekindled

#9 Where She Belongs

#10 Shelter in His Arms

#11 Where Love Stands

About The Author

Tara Baisden is a Contemporary Christian Inspirational Romance author who proudly calls the beautiful state of West Virginia her home. Nestled on a sprawling mountainous property, she is surrounded by the peace and serenity of nature. Her days are happily spent in the quiet of country life, writing heartwarming stories of love, faith, and second chances. Tara also enjoys quilting, working in her garden, tending to her beloved pets, and soaking in the beauty of her surroundings.

With deep roots in West Virginia, family is everything to Tara. One of her favorite pastimes is gathering on the front porch with loved ones, sharing stories, laughter, and enjoying the simple, meaningful moments that life offers. When she's not crafting her novels, Tara can often be found exploring the rich history of her home state, visiting local historical sites, and, of course, stopping by every bookstore she passes! Her passion for reading and discovery always fuels her next adventure.

Tara is the author of the Laurel Ridges series of novels, as well as the Riverbend Valley series of novels, of which have been beloved by fans of inspirational romance. Her novels reflect her love for faith, family, and the timeless beauty of the world we live in.

Known for her sweet and clean romances, she creates characters that feel like family and settings that make readers want to visit again and again.

You can find out more about Tara and her latest releases at www.tarabaisden.com or follow her on social media for updates and behind-the-scenes glimpses of her writing process. Stay connected—you won't want to miss the heartfelt stories of love and family she has in store!

About Laurel Ridge

Welcome to the fictional town of Laurel Ridge, West Virginia!

Nestled deep in the heart of the Appalachian Mountains, Laurel Ridge is a place where time slows down, allowing visitors and residents alike to enjoy life's simple pleasures. With its quaint, brick-paved streets, historic storefronts, and the ever-present backdrop of rolling hills and dense forests, Laurel Ridge is a hidden gem that attracts tourists looking for both serenity and adventure.

A Rich History

The town was founded in the early 1800s by pioneering settlers who were drawn to the fertile land and abundant natural resources of the region. Laurel Ridge began as a small logging community, relying on the towering forests that covered the surrounding mountains. The New River, one of the oldest rivers in the world, provided an essential transportation route for lumber, as well as a lifeline for the early settlers.

As the years passed, the town evolved from a logging outpost into a thriving hub for craftspeople and artisans. By the late 19th century, it had developed a reputation for its hand-crafted furniture, textiles, and pottery, all made by skilled locals. The town's proximity to the New River also made it a destination for adventurous souls seeking to kayak, fish, or hike along the riverbanks.

A Place of Renewal

Though the logging industry faded by the early 20th century, Laurel Ridge adapted to the changing times. Its natural beauty and deep connection to West Virginia's mountain heritage drew travelers from near and far, transforming it into a beloved tourist destination. Local shops, run by generations of the same families, line the town square, offering handmade goods, locally sourced foods, and, most of all, warm hospitality.

The town's signature event, the Harvest Festival, began in the 1930s, celebrating the craftsmanship, music, and traditions passed down through the generations. Each year, visitors flock to enjoy live Appalachian music, taste locally grown produce, and witness demonstrations of old-world techniques like blacksmithing and weaving.

<u>A Town of Faith and Community</u>

At the heart of the town stands Laurel Ridge Community Church, a small, white clapboard building with a steeple that reaches toward the sky. Built in 1876, the church has been a pillar of faith and strength for the community for over a century. Its bell, crafted by the town's original blacksmith, has been ringing on Sunday mornings ever since, calling townsfolk to worship and reminding everyone of the enduring values of faith, hope, and love.

The church's history is intertwined with the town's, serving as a refuge in difficult times and a gathering place in moments of joy. Over the years, the church has grown to include an outreach center that supports local families and tourists in need, providing everything from free meals to spiritual counseling. The church's welcoming atmosphere reflects the town's deep sense of unity and service.

<u>A Growing Tourist Haven</u>

Today, Laurel Ridge has grown to a population of around five thousand people, yet it has managed to retain its small-town charm.

Dedication

To all who have found themselves at unexpected crossroads,
uncertain of the path ahead.
May you discover, as Abby did,
that sometimes coming home isn't about returning to a place,
but about finding where your heart truly belongs.
And to those wrestling with forgiveness—
remember that healing often arrives
in the gentle hands of community,
the warmth of new love,
and the courage to see your story through new eyes.
Love, Tara

Contents

Chapter 1

Abby Marshall's heels clicked across the polished concrete floor of Reed Interiors Incorporated, her stride projecting a confidence that had become second nature after years of navigating Charleston's elite design circles. The sleek office hummed with the familiar energy of a Monday morning, phones ringing, the espresso machine hissing in the kitchenette, junior designers hunched over drafting tables.

"Ms. Marshall?" Her assistant, Penny, appeared at her elbow, tablet in hand. "The Saunders are waiting in the conference room. I've put out the material samples you requested, and Rachel just finished setting up the presentation."

"Perfect. Coffee?"

"Already on the table. Ethiopian blend, black."

Abby smiled. "What would I do without you?"

"Let's hope you never have to find out," Penny replied with a wink.

Taking a deep breath, Abby smoothed her tailored navy dress and mentally shifted into presentation mode. The Saunders were potentially her biggest clients yet, a power couple looking to renovate their historic home on South Battery Street. Landing their project would further her career and reputation as one of Charleston, South Carolina's premier designers.

She opened the conference room door with a practiced smile. "Good morning! I hope I haven't kept you waiting."

Harold Saunders, a silver-haired man with the confident posture of old money, rose to greet her. "Not at all. We were just admiring your portfolio." He gestured to the leather-bound book his wife was flipping through.

Margaret Saunders looked up, her critical gaze taking in Abby's appearance. "Your work for the Prescott's was impressive."

"Thank you." Abby settled into her chair. "Their home presented similar challenges as yours, balancing historic preservation with modern functionality."

For the next hour, Abby led them through her vision for their renovation, presenting mood boards, material samples, and digital renderings with the polished expertise that had become her hallmark. She answered their questions with confident authority, steering them gently when their ideas strayed into impractical territory.

"The kitchen is my primary concern," Margaret said, tapping a manicured nail against the rendering. "I entertain frequently, and the current layout is completely insufficient."

"I thoroughly agree." Abby pulled up an alternative design. "I'm proposing we remove this non-load-bearing wall to open the space, install custom cabinetry along this wall, and create an island that doubles as a prep space and serving area when you host."

Harold nodded approvingly. "You've clearly done your homework on the property."

"I believe in thorough research. Your home deserves nothing less than meticulous attention to every detail."

By the time the meeting concluded, Abby had them nodding along with her recommendations, their initial reservations transformed into enthusiasm.

"We'd like to move forward," Harold announced, extending his hand. "Your vision aligns perfectly with what we're hoping to achieve."

"Wonderful." Abby's smile widened with genuine pleasure. "I'm thrilled to work with you both."

After escorting them out, she returned to her office, closing the door with a satisfied sigh. Another win. Another step toward the recognition she'd worked so hard to achieve. Her gaze drifted to the small collection of design awards displayed on her credenza, tangible proof that she belonged in this world of elegance and sophistication.

Her phone buzzed with a text from Rachel, her junior designer: You nailed it! They couldn't stop raving about you on their way out.

Abby smiled, allowing herself a moment of pride before turning to her computer to catch up on emails. The day stretched ahead with its usual parade of client meetings, vendor calls, and design decisions. By lunchtime, she was deep in conversation with a fabric supplier about a delayed shipment when Penny appeared at her door, face unnaturally pale.

"Abby? David needs to see everyone in the main conference room. Immediately."

Something in Penny's tone made Abby's stomach tighten. "Did he say what it's about?"

"No, but..." Penny hesitated. "The firm's legal team is here."

Abby set down her phone, a cold prickle of unease traveling up her spine. David Reed rarely called impromptu meetings, and the presence of lawyers was unprecedented. She followed Penny to the conference room, where a tense silence had already settled over her colleagues.

David stood at the head of the table, his usual confident demeanor replaced by something Abby had never seen before, defeat. The gray-suited lawyers flanking him looked grim.

"Thank you all for coming so quickly," David began, his voice strained. "I wish I had better news, but I believe in transparency. As of this morning, Reed Interiors Incorporated is filing for Chapter 7 bankruptcy."

The words hit Abby like a physical blow. Bankruptcy? How was that possible? The firm had a solid client base, prestigious projects, and a stellar reputation.

"Unfortunately, the economic downturn hit us harder than anticipated," David continued. "Several major commercial clients have pulled out of projects, and others have fallen behind on payments. Our operating expenses have continued to rise, and despite our best efforts to secure additional financing..." His voice faltered. "We've exhausted all options."

The room erupted in confused murmurs and shocked exclamations. Abby sat frozen, her mind racing to process the implications. Chapter 7 meant liquidation, not restructuring, not a second chance. Complete dissolution.

"What about our current projects?" someone asked.

"We'll be contacting clients today to explain the situation. The court will appoint a trustee to oversee the liquidation of assets and outstanding accounts."

"And us?" This from Rachel, her voice barely above a whisper.

David's shoulders slumped. "Today will be our last day of operation. HR will meet with each of you individually to discuss final pay and benefits."

The meeting continued, but Abby barely heard the details through the roaring in her ears. Seven years of her life, her creative energy, her identity, all tied to this firm that was now collapsing around her. She'd joined as a junior designer fresh out of design school, working her way up to partner through sheer determination and talent. Reed Interiors wasn't just her employer; it was her professional home.

After the meeting, Abby returned to her office on autopilot, closing the door before sinking into her chair. The Saunders project, gone. All her ongoing work, gone. Her salary, her benefits, her professional standing, all in jeopardy. How had she not seen this coming?

A knock at her door interrupted her spiraling thoughts.

"Come in," she called, quickly composing her expression.

David entered, looking ten years older than he had that morning. "Abby, do you have a minute?"

"Of course."

He sat heavily in the chair across from her desk. "I wanted to speak with you personally. You deserve that much."

"What happened, David? Really?"

He sighed, rubbing his temples. "The truth? A perfect storm. The Wilson Tower project, our largest account, went under when their financing fell through. Then the pandemic hit commercial real estate hard. We were already running thin margins to stay competitive." He met her eyes directly. "I should have been more transparent about how precarious things were getting. I kept hoping we'd turn it around."

"I'm a partner. I should have been more aware."

"You were doing your job brilliantly, bringing in clients, delivering exceptional work. The financial side was my responsibility." He paused. "For what it's worth, I'm sorry. You're the most talented designer I've ever worked with. You'll land on your feet."

But as David left, and the day progressed into a blur of HR meetings, boxing personal items, and stunned goodbyes to colleagues, Abby wasn't so sure. Her reputation was now tied to a bankrupt firm. Her savings, while substantial, wouldn't last indefinitely in Charleston's expensive housing market. And the design industry was tight knit. Word would spread quickly.

By evening, Abby sat alone in her downtown apartment, a bottle of sparkling water untouched beside her as she scrolled through her contacts, considering whom to call. Friends in the industry? They'd be sympathetic, but also potential competitors for the limited design positions in Charleston. Family? She had none, apart from distant cousins she barely knew.

Her gaze fell on the framed photo on her coffee table, Aunt Gertrude standing proudly in front of the Victorian house in Laurel Ridge, her arm around a teenage Abby. It had been taken the summer before Abby left for college, her ticket out of the small West Virginia town that held too many painful memories.

Aunt Gertrude had passed away two years ago, leaving Abby the house and a sizable financial inheritance. She'd been putting off dealing with it, too busy with work to take time off. Now, with no job tethering her to Charleston...

"No," she muttered. "Absolutely not."

But as the evening wore on, and she researched job opportunities, calculated her finances, and faced the reality of her situation, the idea took root. The house was a valuable asset, especially with the growing market for vacation properties in scenic mountain towns. With her design expertise, she could renovate it to maximize its value, then sell it and use the proceeds to start her own design firm.

Six months in Laurel Ridge. That's all it would take. Six months to renovate, list the property, and return to Charleston with more than enough capital to rebuild her career on her own terms. It was a practical solution to her sudden financial uncertainty.

It had nothing to do with running back to the comfort of Aunt Gertrude's memory. Nothing to do with retreating from failure. This was a strategic business decision, she told herself firmly.

By midnight, she had sketched out a preliminary plan. By morning, she had made up her mind.

Chapter 2

Three days later, Abby's silver BMW wound through the mountains of West Virginia, leaving the interstate behind for the narrower, twisting roads that led to Laurel Ridge. The late April landscape was a riot of fresh green color, with dogwoods and redbuds dotting the forest in bursts of white and pink. It was beautiful in a wild, untamed way, so different from Charleston's manicured elegance.

As the miles between her and South Carolina increased, Abby felt the knot in her chest both tightening and loosening in contradictory ways. Leaving the city meant leaving behind the humiliation of the firm's collapse, the pitying looks, the awkward encounters with former clients. But it also meant retreating from everything she'd built for herself, her sophisticated social circle, her reputation as a rising star in design, and the urban lifestyle she'd embraced.

And it meant returning to Laurel Ridge, a place that held as much pain as comfort in her memories.

Her phone, connected to the car's Bluetooth, rang through the speakers. Leslie's name appeared on the dashboard display.

"Hey," Abby answered, grateful for the distraction from her thoughts.

"Where are you?"

Abby smiled despite herself. Leslie Williams had been her closest friend growing up, and despite the distance and time that had separated them, they'd maintained their connection through calls, texts, and occasional visits.

"About twenty minutes out, I think. Traffic was lighter than expected."

"I can't wait to see you!" Leslie's enthusiasm bubbled through the speakers. "I've aired out the house as best I could, but it's been vacant since..." Her voice softened. "Well, you know."

"I appreciate it, Les. Really."

"Are you okay?" Leslie asked, her tone shifting to concern. "And don't give me the polished Charleston version. It's me you're talking to."

Abby sighed, keeping her eyes on the winding road. "I'm...processing. One day, I'm pitching to my biggest client yet, the next I'm unemployed, and my professional reputation is potentially in tatters. It's been a week, let me tell ya."

"Your reputation is built on your talent, not the firm. This is a setback, not the end." Leslie paused. "Maybe it's even an opportunity."

"That's precisely how I'm approaching it," Abby replied, her voice firming with resolve. "Six months to renovate Aunt Gertrude's house, sell it at a profit, and launch my own design business. A strategic reset."

"Mmm-hmm. And it has nothing to do with coming home and maybe staying?"

"Laurel Ridge isn't home, Les. It hasn't been for a long time."

The silence on the other end spoke volumes.

"Anyway," Abby continued, "I should be there soon. Are you sure you can't meet me at the house?"

"I wish I could, but we've got three wedding consultations back-to-back today. Spring is insane for the flower business. But I've left a welcome basket on the kitchen counter, and I'll come by as soon as I close up shop. Around six?"

"That sounds perfect. Thanks, Leslie."

As she ended the call, Abby rounded a bend in the road and caught her first glimpse of Laurel Ridge nestled in the valley below. The small town was cradled by the rolling Appalachian hills, its church steeple rising above the treeline, the town square a patch of green at its center. From this distance, it looked like a picture postcard, quaint, charming, and untouched by time.

Abby's hands tightened on the steering wheel as she descended into the valley. Twelve years since she'd left for college, returning only for brief visits, usually at Christmas when Aunt Gertrude insisted. Now she was back, not as a visitor, but as a temporary resident. The thought sent a nervous flutter through her stomach.

The road led her past the "Welcome to Laurel Ridge" sign, with its population count of 4,457, nearly the same as when she'd left. Main Street appeared ahead, lined with brick storefronts and planters bursting with spring flowers. The town square came into view, the white gazebo at its center surrounded by benches and blooming dogwood trees.

Abby slowed, taking in the familiar sights. Martha's Diner, where she and Leslie had spent countless hours during high school. The Book Nook, where she'd hidden away on rainy afternoons. Laurel Ridge Community Church, where Aunt Gertrude had taken her every Sunday without fail.

And then, as she turned onto Maple Avenue, she saw it, the Marshall Victorian. Rising three stories on its hillside perch, it overlooked the town with an air of faded grandeur. The cream and pale green paint were peeling in places, the gardens overgrown, but even in its neglected state, the house possessed an undeniable charm and dignity.

Uncle Wilburn, a respected architect, had lovingly maintained the historic home until his death fourteen years ago. After that, Aunt Gertrude had done her best, until age and limited mobility had made upkeep difficult. The house had been too much for one elderly woman, but she'd refused to leave the home she'd shared with her husband for multiple years.

Abby parked in the curved driveway and sat for a moment, gathering herself. This house had been her salvation once, the place where Aunt Gertrude and Uncle Wilburn had taken her in after her parents abandoned her, giving her stability, love, and a chance at a normal life. Now it represented her financial salvation.

"It's just a house," she reminded herself. "A project. An asset."

But as she climbed the porch steps, each creak familiar beneath her feet, and slipped the key into the lock, emotions she'd long suppressed threatened to surface. The door swung open with a groan, revealing the grand foyer with its sweeping staircase and crystal chandelier.

The scent hit her immediately, a mixture of furniture polish, old books, and something distinctly Gertrude, a faint whisper of lavender and talcum powder. For an instant, Abby half-expected to hear her aunt's warm voice calling a greeting from the kitchen.

Instead, silence greeted her.

"Hello, old friend," she murmured, her voice echoing slightly in the empty space.

Abby moved through the rooms, taking mental notes of necessary repairs and updates. The formal living room with its elegant fireplace and built-in bookshelves. The dining room with the mahogany table where they'd shared countless meals. The kitchen, desperately outdated with its vintage appliances and worn linoleum floor.

Everywhere she looked, she saw the signs of neglect that accompanied an aging owner's declining health, alongside touches of the home's former beauty. It would be a substantial project to bring the house back to its former glory, but that's what she did best, transforming spaces, revealing hidden potential, and creating beauty from neglect.

This was just another project. A temporary stay in a place she'd once called home, a strategic business move. Nothing more.

Upstairs, Abby hesitated outside her old bedroom before pushing the door open. Unlike the rest of the house, this room looked frozen in time. The twin bed with its patchwork quilt. The desk where she'd studied for hours, determined to earn a scholarship. The bulletin board still pinned with college acceptance letters, design magazine cutouts, and photos of her with Leslie at high school events.

She sat on the edge of the bed, running her hand over the familiar quilt. Aunt Gertrude had kept it exactly as she'd left it, as though expecting her to return someday. The thought sent an unexpected pang through her chest.

Focus, Abby. This is a business decision, not a homecoming.

Her phone buzzed with a text from her moving company, informing her they'd be arriving within the hour with her belongings from Charleston. The message provided the push she needed to snap back into practical mode.

Making her way back downstairs, she found Leslie's welcome basket on the kitchen counter, fresh flowers from her shop, homemade cookies, locally roasted coffee, and a bottle of sparkling cider. The attached note read: "Welcome back! Even temporary residents deserve to feel at home. Can't wait to catch up. Love, Leslie."

Abby smiled, touched by the gesture. If there was one bright spot about returning to Laurel Ridge, it was reconnecting with Leslie's unwavering friendship.

Standing alone in the kitchen where Aunt Gertrude had taught her to bake, surrounded by memories that pressed in from all sides. Abby couldn't shake the feeling that her aunt was still with her, even though she'd been gone for two years now.

Not ghosts, she told herself firmly. Just memories. And memories couldn't hurt her, couldn't judge her, couldn't remind her that she was the abandoned girl from the trailer park who never quite belonged, even in a town where everyone knew her name.

She moved to the window, looking out at the overgrown garden and, beyond it, the rolling hills and the small-town below. Somewhere in those hills were the remains of the trailer where she'd lived until age ten, where her parents had left her alone for days. Somewhere in that town were people who remembered her not as the successful Charleston designer, but as "that poor Marshall girl."

"Six months," she whispered to herself, her breath fogging the glass. "Renovate, sell, and move on. Again."

But as the afternoon light filtered through the trees, casting dappled shadows across the yard that had once been her safe haven, a small voice deep inside, one that sounded suspiciously like Aunt Gertrude, whispered back: *What if this time, moving on isn't the answer?*

Abby straightened her shoulders and turned away from the window. She had a house to renovate, a career to rebuild, and a life waiting for her back in Charleston. That was the plan, and she was sticking to it.

Starting tomorrow, she would contact local contractors about the renovation. She'd map out a comprehensive plan, create a budget, and execute it with the same precision and vision that had made her successful in Charleston. This wasn't about coming home; it was about using her skills to create a foundation for her next professional chapter.

Yet as she walked through the rooms of the grand old house, making notes on her tablet and deliberately focusing on the practical aspects of the project ahead. She couldn't quite silence the whisper of something deeper stirring beneath her carefully constructed composure.

Maybe Leslie's right. A voice nudged. *Perhaps this setback is an opportunity, just not the kind you're thinking.*

"Stop it," she muttered to herself. "Stay focused."

But the Marshall Victorian had always had a way of working into her heart, of making her feel both vulnerable and safe. And as the moving truck pulled up outside and the reality of her situation sank in, Abby wondered if six months in Laurel Ridge might change more than just the house.

She pushed the thought aside. She was here for one reason only: to renovate this house, sell it, and return to the life she'd built. Anything else was simply nostalgia, and nostalgia was a luxury she couldn't afford. Not when her entire professional future hung in the balance.

The movers began bringing in boxes labeled with her neat handwriting, "Kitchen," "Bedroom," "Office Supplies." Each one a piece of her Charleston life, now temporarily transplanted to this place of her past. The juxtaposition felt jarring, like worlds colliding that were never meant to meet.

As the afternoon wore on and the house gradually filled with her belongings, Abby felt an odd sensation of being caught between two lives, the sophisticated Charleston designer and the small-town girl she'd once been. The feeling wasn't entirely comfortable, but she reminded herself it was temporary. Just like her stay in Laurel Ridge.

By the time the movers left, and the sun began to set, Abby had unpacked enough to make the house livable. She was arranging her design books on a shelf in the living room when a knock at the door startled her.

Opening it, she found Leslie standing on the porch, holding a pizza box and wearing the same warm smile Abby remembered from childhood.

"I figured you wouldn't have cooked," Leslie said, stepping forward to envelop Abby in a hug before she could respond. "Gosh, it's good to see you."

Abby returned the embrace, surprised by the sudden tightness in her throat. "You too."

Leslie pulled back, her eyes taking in Abby's appearance. "Still the picture of elegance, I see. Meanwhile, I've got potting soil under my nails and probably look like I've been wrestling with my inventory."

"You look perfect," Abby said sincerely. Leslie's wavy auburn hair was pulled back in a messy ponytail, her jeans had smudges of dirt, and she smelled faintly of flowers and earth, completely at ease in her own skin in a way Abby had always admired.

"Come in. I was just about to open the sparkling cider you left for me."

"Now you're talking." Leslie followed her into the kitchen, setting the pizza on the counter. "So, how does it feel to be back?"

Abby busied herself opening the bottle of cider from Leslie's welcome basket. "Surreal. Everything's so familiar, but different too."

"That's small towns for you. Change happens, but at a glacial pace." Leslie accepted the glass Abby handed her. "The biggest news since you were last here is that Pastor Whitman got married."

"The new pastor?"

"Andrew Whitman. Took over about a year ago when Pastor Thompson retired. He's younger, mid-thirties, and brings a fresh perspective. His wife, Lily, is lovely. She's started a community garden behind the church."

Abby nodded politely. Church was low on her priority list for her temporary stay. She opened the pizza box, grateful to find it was still hot. "How's business at the flower shop?"

"Blooming," Leslie grinned at her own pun. "Seriously, though, it's good. I've expanded into event planning, which pairs naturally with the rest of my business. Keeps me busy."

They settled at the kitchen table with their pizza, falling into the easy conversation of old friends. Leslie filled her in on town gossip, who had married, who had moved away, and which businesses had changed hands.

"Oh, and you'll need to meet Mike Hatfield," Leslie said between bites. "He runs Hatfield House Doctors. He's the best contractor in town. If you're serious about renovating, he's your guy."

"I'll add him to my list. I want to start getting quotes as soon as possible."

Leslie studied her over the rim of her glass. "You're really serious about the six-month timeline, aren't you?"

"I have to be. I need to capitalize on the fall selling season, and I can't afford to be away from Charleston any longer than necessary if I want to launch my own firm."

"And what if you find you like it here?"

Abby laughed, though it sounded strained even to her own ears. "Leslie, I appreciate the thought, but let's be realistic. Laurel Ridge is a lovely place to visit, but there's no market here for high-end interior design. My life is in Charleston."

"Is it?" Leslie's gaze was gentle but direct. "You just lost your job, Abby. Maybe this is a chance to reevaluate what you really want."

Abby tensed. "What I want is to rebuild my career. This setback doesn't change that."

Sensing her resistance, Leslie changed the subject. "Well, whatever your plans, I'm selfishly glad to have you here, even temporarily. I've missed you."

The simple honesty in her friend's voice melted some of Abby's defensiveness. "I've missed you too."

They continued talking as the evening deepened, catching up on the years spent apart. Despite her determination to keep an emotional distance from Laurel Ridge, Abby found herself relaxing in Leslie's company, laughing at her stories and feeling, just for moments at a time, like she belonged.

When Leslie left with promises to check in tomorrow, Abby stood on the porch watching her friend's taillights disappear down the winding driveway. The night was alive with sounds she'd forgotten, crickets chirping, the distant hoot of an owl, the rustle of leaves in the gentle breeze. So different from Charleston's urban hum of traffic and nightlife.

Re-entering the house, she was struck anew by its emptiness. Not just the absence of people, but the stillness that spoke of Aunt Gertrude's absence. The house felt like it was waiting, holding its breath.

"Stop it," she chided herself. "Houses don't have feelings."

Yet as she climbed the stairs to her old bedroom, carrying a glass of water and her tablet loaded with preliminary renovation plans. Abby couldn't shake the feeling that the Marshall Victorian was more than just a structure of wood and stone. It was a repository of memories, both painful and precious, and it had drawn her back at a moment when she was most vulnerable.

Sitting cross-legged on her childhood bed, she began making notes for the renovation, updated kitchen and bathrooms, restored hardwood floors, fresh paint inside and out, and landscaping to tame the overgrown gardens. Practical tasks. Measurable progress. This was what she needed to focus on, not nebulous feelings about belonging or questioning her life choices.

Outside her window, the mountains loomed as dark silhouettes against the night sky, steadfast and unchanging. Laurel Ridge slumbered below, its lights twinkling like earthbound stars. And somewhere in that landscape of past and present, Abby Marshall, successful designer, determined professional, and secretly terrified woman, would find her path forward.

Six months. That was the plan. Renovate, sell, return to Charleston.

But as she set aside her tablet and prepared for bed, a small voice inside whispered that plans, like houses, sometimes needed unexpected renovation themselves.

Chapter 3

The morning sun had barely cleared the mountain ridges when Abby pushed open the door to Martha's Diner, greeted by the cheerful jingle of the bell above the door and the rich aroma of coffee and bacon. After a restless night, she'd woken early with a growling stomach and the realization that the kitchen contained nothing but Leslie's welcome basket and leftover pizza.

Martha's Diner hadn't changed. The black-and-white checkered floor, red vinyl booths, and chrome-trimmed counter transported Abby back to her high school days. Even the jukebox in the corner looked identical, though it had probably been updated to include music from this decade.

"Well, I'll be!" a familiar voice rang out. "Abigail Marshall, as I live and breathe!"

Martha Kincaid emerged from behind the counter, dish towel in hand and a wide smile lighting her face. In her sixties now, Martha still had the same energetic presence, though her once-dark hair was completely silver. She wore a blue apron over a simple dress, a small gold cross necklace glinting at her throat.

"Martha," Abby smiled, genuinely pleased to see the woman who had fed her countless meals during her youth. "It's good to see you."

"Let me look at you," Martha said, placing her hands on Abby's shoulders and studying her face. "Still beautiful as ever, but too thin! City living doesn't feed the soul like home cooking."

Before Abby could respond, Martha was steering her toward a booth by the window. "Sit, sit! Coffee's coming right up... still take it black with just a touch of sugar?"

Abby blinked in surprise. "You remember how I take my coffee?"

Martha winked. "Honey, I remember everyone's order. It's my superpower." She patted Abby's hand. "Now, you sit tight. I'm bringing you the works. You look like you need it."

As Martha bustled away, Abby felt a rush of unexpected warmth. She'd forgotten this about small towns, the way people remembered the details of your life, kept them safe, like treasures to be brought out when you returned.

The diner was about half-full, mostly with people grabbing breakfast before work. A couple of heads turned when she entered, and she caught the flicker of recognition in their eyes. She straightened her posture instinctively, smoothing her cream silk blouse. First impressions mattered, even when you were returning to a place where people thought they already knew you.

Martha returned with a steaming mug of coffee, setting it down with a motherly smile. "So, you're back to fix up Gertrude's place?"

"Yes," Abby clarified, wrapping her fingers around the warm ceramic. "Just long enough to renovate and sell it."

"Well, that old house could use some TLC. Gertrude did her best, but that last year was hard on her."

"I know." A twinge of guilt pinched at Abby. She should have visited more often during Aunt Gertrude's decline, but work had always seemed so pressing. "I'm hoping to restore it to its former glory and give it a fresh look before listing it."

"Well, you picked the right season for it. Spring into summer is when Laurel Ridge really shines." Martha's gaze softened. "Your aunt would be happy to see you here, you know. She was always so proud of you."

The sincerity in Martha's voice caught Abby off guard. She took a sip of coffee to mask her sudden emotion. "Thanks, Martha."

"Now, who are you thinking of hiring for the work? That old Victorian will need a skilled hand."

"Actually, I was hoping you might have some recommendations. Leslie mentioned someone named Mike Hatfield?"

Martha's eyes lit up. "Mike! Oh honey, he's the absolute best. Hatfield House Doctors... clever name, isn't it? That boy can fix anything with two hands and a toolbox. Plus, he's honest as the day is long."

"Sounds good."

"And his work is impeccable. He renovated the library last year, your uncle Wilburn's original design, you know, and preserved all the historical details." Martha leaned in slightly. "Plus, he's not hard on the eyes."

Abby raised an eyebrow. "I'm hiring a contractor, Martha, not looking for a date."

Martha laughed, a rich, warm sound. "Of course, dear. Professional all the way." She winked. "But I'm just saying, a nice view never hurt anybody during a renovation. He's about your age."

The bell above the door jingled, and Leslie rushed in, auburn curls bouncing.

"Abby!" She slid into the booth opposite Abby. "Morning, Martha. Coffee, please? The strongest you've got?"

"Coming right up, sweetheart." Martha squeezed Leslie's shoulder affectionately before heading back to the counter.

"Sorry, I'm late," Leslie said, unwinding a floral scarf from her neck. "Early delivery of Dutch tulips needed processing before they wilted."

"I didn't know we were meeting," Abby said, genuinely confused.

Leslie grinned. "We weren't officially, but I figured you'd end up here for breakfast. First rule of small towns... anticipate movements based on limited options."

"Am I that predictable?"

"Well, you've never been one for grocery shopping. And second, Laurel Ridge has no grocery delivery service. So, process of elimination."

Abby laughed.

"So," Leslie said, accepting the coffee Martha brought her with a grateful smile, "what's the plan for today?"

"Finding a contractor. Your suggestion is looking promising. Martha also recommended Mike Hatfield."

"Told you." Leslie stirred a generous amount of cream into her coffee. "Mike's the best. Did Martha mention he's single?" She waggled her eyebrows playfully.

"Oh for—" Abby rolled her eyes. "Are you and Martha in cahoots? I'm not interested in dating anyone in Laurel Ridge. I'm here to renovate and leave, remember?"

"Can't blame a girl for trying. This town could use some good gossip." Leslie's tone was light, but her eyes were observant. "Seriously, though, Mike is perfect for the job. His company specializes in older homes, and he's passionate about preserving historical elements."

Martha arrived with Abby's breakfast, a plate heaped with scrambled eggs, bacon, and biscuits smothered in gravy. "Eat up, honey. You're going to need your strength to renovate that big old house."

"This looks wonderful, Martha, but it's far too much."

"Nonsense. You Charleston girls probably think a leaf of kale is breakfast. Here, we believe in starting the day right."

As Martha moved away to tend to other customers, Leslie leaned forward. "She's right, you know. The Marshall house is a big undertaking."

"I'm aware," Abby said, cutting into her eggs. "But I've managed larger commercial projects. This is just a house."

"It's not just a house," Leslie's voice softened. "It's a piece of Laurel Ridge history. And your history."

Abby paused, fork halfway to her mouth. "It's an asset that needs updating before sale. That's all."

Leslie tilted her head, studying Abby with a look that said she wasn't buying it. "If you say so. Anyway, Mike's office is just a few doors down, right next to the antique store. You should head over after breakfast."

"I was planning to call for an appointment."

"This is Laurel Ridge, Abby. We don't stand on ceremony here." Leslie glanced at her watch. "I've got to run, wedding consultation in twenty minutes. But text me later? Maybe we can have dinner at my place tonight?"

"Sure." Abby watched as Leslie gulped down the rest of her coffee, threw some cash on the table, and rushed out with a wave, her floral-patterned sundress swirling around her knees.

After finishing what she could of Martha's generous breakfast, Abby paid her bill, leaving a generous tip, and stepped back onto Main Street. The morning air was crisp and clear, the kind of quality you never experience in the city. She took a deep breath, unconsciously straightening her shoulders before heading in the direction of Hatfield House Doctors.

Chapter 4

The office wasn't hard to find. It was a small, modest storefront with a wooden sign hanging above the door. The display window showcased several before-and-after photographs of renovation projects, all impressive transformations of older homes. Abby studied them with a professional eye, noting the attention to detail and the respect for original architectural elements.

A bell chimed as she pushed open the door. The front office was small but organized, with a reception desk, a few chairs, and walls lined with framed photographs of completed projects. Numerous architectural drawings were displayed alongside samples of wood finishes, tile options, and hardware.

No one was at the reception desk, but she could hear movement from a room beyond. "Hello?" she called.

A crash followed by muffled muttering answered her. A moment later, a man emerged from the back room, rubbing his shoulder.

"Sorry about that," he said, his deep voice carrying a soft mountain accent. "Knocked into the shelf. You caught me by surprise."

Abby's first thought was that Martha hadn't been exaggerating. Mike Hatfield was certainly not hard on the eyes. Tall, broad-shouldered, with dark hair that fell slightly over his forehead, and warm hazel eyes that regarded her with momentary surprise before settling into polite attentiveness. He wore a simple Henley shirt that stretched across his chest, jeans that had clearly seen honest work, and work boots. His hands, she noted, were large and calloused, working hands, capable and strong.

"I apologize for dropping in unannounced," she said, extending her hand. "I'm Abby Marshall. I was told you might be able to help with renovating the Marshall Victorian."

Something flickered in his eyes. Recognition, perhaps, but it was gone so quickly she might have imagined it. He wiped his hand on his jeans before taking hers in a firm but gentle handshake.

"Mike Hatfield. It's a pleasure to meet you, Ms. Marshall." His handshake was warm and steady, though she noticed a slight hesitation before he released her hand. "Please, have a seat."

He gestured to a small seating area with two chairs and a coffee table spread with home renovation magazines. As she sat, smoothing her pants, she noticed him subtly straightening his shirt and running a hand through his hair.

"So, the Marshall place," he said, taking the seat across from her. "Quite a property. One of Wilburn's finest designs, if you don't mind me saying."

"You know my uncle's work?" Abby asked, genuinely surprised.

A small smile lifted the corner of his mouth. "Everyone in Laurel Ridge knows Wilburn Marshall's work. He designed half the important buildings in town. I actually studied architectural design for a while before focusing on the restoration and construction side of things."

There was a quiet passion in his voice when he spoke about architecture that Abby found unexpectedly appealing. It reminded her of her own enthusiasm when discussing design concepts with clients.

"I'm looking to renovate the house and then put it up for sale," she explained, pulling a tablet from her bag. "I'd like to preserve its historical character while updating key areas to appeal to modern buyers."

Mike nodded, listening attentively as she outlined her initial plans—modernizing the kitchen and bathrooms, restoring the hardwood floors, updating the electrical and plumbing systems, and addressing the exterior paint and landscaping.

"That's a substantial project," he said when she finished. "Mind if I ask about your timeline?"

"Three months, maximum, for the restoration. Then the next three months to sell it. This timeframe gives a bit of a cushion if the restoration takes a little longer than projected. But I'd like to list it as soon as possible."

His eyebrows rose slightly. "That's... ambitious, given the scope of work you're describing."

"I'm on a deadline," she said firmly. "I need to get back to Charleston by fall to launch my own interior design firm."

Mike seemed to consider this, his expression thoughtful. "Well, if anyone can make it happen, it'd be someone with your background," he said, surprising her. When she looked questioningly at him, he added, "I've heard about your work. Charleston's design scene makes the regional journals, and Leslie mentioned you were a partner at Reed Interiors."

Abby felt a flutter of professional pride, followed immediately by the sting of the firm's collapse. "Was being the operative word," she said, keeping her tone even. "The firm recently went under, which is partly why I'm here now."

Mike's expression shifted to one of genuine sympathy. "I'm sorry to hear that. Business closures are tough."

His sincerity caught her off guard, and she found herself responding more honestly than she'd intended. "It was unexpected. One day, I was pitching to clients, and then later that afternoon I was packing up my office."

"That's rough," he said simply, no pity in his voice, just quiet understanding.

An awkward silence stretched between them until he cleared his throat. "Would you like to schedule a time for me to come out and take a proper look at the house? I'd need to assess the structure, systems, and any potential challenges before giving you an accurate estimate."

"Yes, of course." Abby was grateful for the return to business. "When are you available?"

"I could stop by tomorrow morning if that works for you? Around nine?"

"That would be perfect."

Mike nodded, making a note in a leather-bound planner. "I'll bring my assessment checklist, take some measurements. Nothing invasive for this first visit."

As he wrote, Abby studied him more carefully. There was something vaguely familiar about him, though she couldn't place it. "Have we met before?"

Mike looked up, a flicker of something—disappointment?—crossing his face so quickly she couldn't be certain. "Uh, well, we went to Laurel Ridge High at the same time, actually. I was a year ahead of you."

Abby blinked, surprised. "Oh, I'm sorry, I don't..."

"No reason you should remember," he said quickly, his smile self-deprecating. "I was pretty quiet back then. Still am, I guess. But I did some work for your aunt about a year before she passed, fixed her roof after a big storm."

"Oh, right," Abby said, though in truth, she had no recollection of Aunt Gertrude mentioning it.

Another small silence fell, this one more awkward than the last. Mike stood, and Abby followed suit.

"Well, I appreciate your time today," she said, extending her hand again. "I'll see you tomorrow at nine."

"Looking forward to it." He shook her hand, his grip warm and firm. This time, she noticed tiny scars on his knuckles, the battle wounds of his trade, she supposed.

Back outside on the sidewalk, Abby paused, taking in the peaceful bustle of Laurel Ridge's main street. Across the way, a young mother was pushing a stroller, an elderly couple walked hand in hand, and a man was sweeping the sidewalk in front of the hardware store. It was like a scene from a small-town tourism brochure.

Yet beneath the picture-perfect exterior, Abby sensed undercurrents she'd forgotten about, the way information traveled like electricity through the community grapevine, the weight of family names and histories. The unspoken expectation that who you had been would always define who you were.

She wondered what Mike Hatfield remembered about her from high school. The scholarship student from the wrong side of town? The orphaned girl taken in by her aunt and uncle? Or worse, the standoffish teenager who couldn't wait to escape Laurel Ridge?

Shaking off the uncomfortable thoughts, Abby headed toward her car. She had a grocery list to make, supplies to buy, and preliminary plans to refine before Mike's visit tomorrow. The renovation was the only thing that mattered now. Everything else, including the unset-tling awareness of Mike Hatfield's warm eyes and capable hands, was irrelevant.

***

Mike stood at the window of his office, watching Abby walk away. She moved with a confidence that hadn't been there in high school, head high, shoulders back, and each step was purposeful. The awkward teenager with determined eyes had transformed into a polished, sophisticated woman who looked like she belonged on the glossy pages of the design magazines on his coffee table.

And she didn't remember him at all.

He shouldn't be surprised. Back in high school, he'd been painfully shy around girls, especially Abby Marshall. He'd admired her from afar, her determination, her intelligence, the quiet dignity with which she'd carried herself despite the whispers about her parents. They'd had exactly two conversations in four years: once when he'd helped her pick up books someone had knocked from her hands, and once during a group project in the only class they'd shared.

"Dad? Earth to Dad!"

Mike turned to find his eight-year-old son, Tyler, standing in the doorway to the back office, a quizzical expression on his face.

"Hey, buddy. Sorry, I was thinking." Mike ruffled his son's dark hair, so similar to his own. "Did Mrs. Perkins drop you off? I didn't hear her car."

"She parked behind the building because there weren't any spaces in front." Tyler peered around Mike toward the window. "Who's that lady? She looks fancy."

Mike guided Tyler back toward the office. "That is Ms. Marshall. She's renovating her aunt's house, the big Victorian on the hill. We might be doing the work."

"The spooky, empty one?" Tyler's eyes widened.

"It's not spooky, it's historic," Mike corrected, though he understood why the old house, with its elaborate Victorian details and overgrown garden, might look imposing to an eight-year-old.

"Is she nice?"

Mike smiled. "Yes, she is nice and very focused on renovating that big mansion."

"Like you, when you're working on blueprints?"

"Something like that." Mike checked his watch. "Hey, we need to get you to baseball practice. Go grab your gear, okay?"

As Tyler scurried off to collect his baseball shoes and water bottle from the small break room where he sometimes did homework after school, Mike allowed himself one more glance out the window. Abby was gone, but the impression she'd left lingered.

Three months for her renovation. Three months to sell. She'd be in Laurel Ridge for at least that amount of time, then gone again. Back to Charleston and the sophisticated world that suited her so well. It was probably for the best that she didn't remember him. This was business, pure and simple.

Still, as he locked up the office and headed to his truck with Tyler chattering beside him, Mike couldn't help but wonder what it would be like to work alongside Abby day after day on the renovation.

As he started the engine and pulled onto Main Street, he found himself looking forward to tomorrow's appointment with an eagerness that had nothing to do with professional opportunities.

"Dad, can we get pizza for dinner?" Tyler asked, buckling his seatbelt.

Mike smiled, grateful for the interruption in his thoughts. "Sure, buddy. Pizza sounds good."

Chapter 5

Mike pulled up to the Marshall home precisely at 8:55 AM. He killed the engine and reached for his worn leather satchel containing a measuring tape, clipboard, digital camera, and inspection checklist. The cool morning air carried the scent of spring, damp earth, budding trees, and the faint sweetness of nearby wildflowers.

The house loomed before him, grand and slightly forlorn. Pale morning light cast long shadows across the wrap-around porch, highlighting peeling paint and sagging steps. Despite its neglected state, the Victorian retained an undeniable dignity. Wilburn Marshall's architectural genius was evident in every graceful line and thoughtful detail. The intricate gingerbread trim, the perfect proportions of the windows, and the dramatic sweep of the roof.

Mike took a deep breath, checking his reflection in the rearview mirror. He'd chosen his most professional work shirt, a crisp navy button-down, though he'd rolled up the sleeves in preparation for the inspection. He'd even trimmed his beard last night, a detail that had made Tyler giggle.

"You look nice, Dad. Is it because of the fancy lady?" his son had asked with an eight-year-old directness.

Mike had muttered something about professional appearances, but Tyler's knowing grin had made him wonder if he was being more transparent than he'd thought.

Shaking off the thought, Mike headed up the walkway. Before he could knock, the front door swung open.

"Right on time," Abby said.

She wore fitted jeans and a simple white button-down shirt with the sleeves rolled to her elbows, practical attire for a house assessment, but she somehow managed to make it look elegant. Her chestnut brown hair was pulled back in a ponytail, revealing the clean lines of her face. No makeup that he could discern, just the natural glow of fair skin and the striking contrast of her dark eyebrows against hazel eyes.

"Good morning," Mike replied, trying not to stare. "Hope I didn't keep you waiting."

"Not at all. I've been up since six making notes." She stepped back, gesturing him inside. "Coffee?"

"That would be great, thanks."

The foyer was exactly as he remembered from his brief visit to repair Gertrude's roof, grand in scale, with high ceilings, dark wainscoting, and a sweeping staircase. Sunlight poured through the stained-glass panel above the front door, casting colored patterns on the hardwood floor.

"Follow me," Abby said, leading him toward the kitchen. "Fair warning. It's a bit of a time capsule back here."

The kitchen was indeed a blast from the past—original cabinetry from what looked like the 1960s, an avocado-green refrigerator, and linoleum flooring printed with a faded geometric pattern. But the space itself was generous, with high ceilings and large windows overlooking the backyard.

Abby poured coffee into two mugs, pushing one toward him across the worn Formica countertop. "Sugar? I'm afraid there's no cream. I haven't done a proper grocery run yet."

"Black is fine," Mike said, taking the mug gratefully. "Thanks."

He noticed a stack of papers covered the kitchen table, floor plans, sketches, and what looked like a detailed inventory of each room.

"You've been busy," he commented.

"I believe in being prepared." She took a sip of her coffee, watching him over the rim. "I spent yesterday afternoon measuring and documenting the existing conditions. I can share my drawings with you if that helps."

"That would be great. Would you prefer to walk with me through each room, or would you rather I give you an overview when I'm finished?"

"Let's walk through together," Abby decided. "I'd like to get your unfiltered reactions to each space."

Mike nodded, appreciating her directness. "Sounds good. Where would you like to start?"

"First floor, then upstairs, finishing with the basement. I've sketched a preliminary plan for each room, but I'm open to your professional assessment regarding what's feasible." She gestured to the surrounding kitchen. "Obviously, this room needs a complete overhaul."

Mike set his coffee down and pulled out his notebook, beginning a careful assessment. "The bones of this kitchen are actually excellent. High ceilings, good natural light, spacious layout. The cabinetry is dated, but solid wood... could be refinished rather than replaced if you're working with budget constraints."

"No," Abby said firmly. "The cabinets need to go. I'm thinking clean white Shaker style, marble or quartz countertops, and a farmhouse sink. We'll need all new appliances, of course."

"Of course," Mike agreed, making notes. He walked over to the sink and turned on the faucet, noting the weak water pressure and the slightly rust-colored water that emerged. "Plumbing will need work. These old galvanized pipes tend to corrode from the inside out. I'd recommend replacing them throughout the house."

"That could be costly," Abby frowned.

"It is, but it's one of those invisible improvements that significantly impacts the home's value. Buyers these days expect good water pressure and clean pipes." Mike kneeled to examine the underside of the sink cabinet, noting water damage and signs of past leaks. "There's been some water damage here, but the floor joists might be okay. We'll know more once we open everything up."

They continued through the first floor, the formal dining room with its ornate built-in china cabinet, the spacious living room with its beautiful but inefficient fireplace, a small study lined with empty bookshelves. And a cramped powder room tucked under the stairs.

In each space, Mike methodically assessed the structural elements, electrical fixtures, windows, and flooring. Abby followed with her tablet, occasionally making notes or asking questions. He could sense her growing appreciation for his thoroughness, and he found himself impressed by her keen eye for design potential.

"The fireplace in the living room is original to the house," Mike said, running his hand along the intricate woodwork of the mantel. "Wilburn Marshall was known for these detailed fireplace surrounds. It's almost like a signature piece."

"It's beautiful," Abby agreed. "But it looks like there's some damage to the hearth."

Mike knelt to examine the cracked tiles. "Good eye. These would need to be replaced, and I'd recommend having the chimney inspected and cleaned. It's probably been years since it was properly maintained."

"Is that something you handle, or would I need to hire a specialist?"

"We work with a certified chimney sweep, so we could coordinate that for you. Same with electrical, plumbing, and HVAC specialists. We bring in licensed professionals as needed, but manage the whole process."

Abby nodded approvingly. "That's helpful. I don't have time to juggle multiple contractors."

In the study, Mike paused in front of the built-in bookshelves, admiring the craftsmanship. "These are extraordinary—hand-carved by the looks of it."

"My uncle's books used to fill them completely," Abby said, her voice softening. "Architecture volumes, engineering manuals, fiction... he was quite the reader."

Mike noted the shift in her tone, a momentary vulnerability that seemed involuntary. "What happened to all the books?"

"Some went to the Laurel Ridge Library after Uncle Wilburn passed. Aunt Gertrude kept his favorites, but I'm not sure where those ended up..." Abby trailed off, then straightened her shoulders. "Anyway, these shelves need refinishing, but are otherwise in good shape."

"They're a real selling point," Mike agreed, sensing her desire to return to business. "Custom built-ins like these would cost a fortune to replicate today."

"That's what I was thinking too," she replied.

As they climbed the stairs to the second floor, Mike noted the solid construction, no creaking or sagging, despite the home's age. "Your uncle built things to last," he commented, running his hand along the smooth banister.

"He believed in quality," Abby replied. "He used to say that good architecture should outlive its creator by centuries."

The upstairs hall was flooded with light from a round window at the end of the corridor. Four-bedroom doors lined the hallway, along with a linen closet and the entrance to what Mike assumed was the main bathroom.

"This was my room," Abby said, pushing open the first door on the right.

The bedroom was modest in size but charming, with a window seat overlooking the front yard and built-in drawers beneath a sloped ceiling section. Faded floral wallpaper covered the walls, and the hardwood floor was partially hidden by a worn area rug.

Mike tried to imagine teenage Abby in this space, doing homework at the small desk by the window, dreaming of escape to bigger cities and brighter futures. The room felt like a time capsule, preserved exactly as she must have left it years ago.

"Good bones in here," he said professionally. "Wallpaper would need to go. Floors refinished. Any specific vision for this room?"

"Nothing too dramatic," Abby said, her voice carefully neutral. "Fresh paint, refinished floors, updated lighting. I'm thinking of staging it as a guest bedroom or home office when I list it."

"Makes sense. The built-in storage is a nice feature."

They moved through the remaining bedrooms, the master suite with its outdated attached bathroom, a smaller bedroom that had clearly been Gertrude's sewing room, and a fourth bedroom that had been converted to storage.

The main bathroom was a design nightmare, pink and black tile, a massive cast iron tub with claw feet, and gaudy gold fixtures.

"This is… something," Mike said diplomatically.

Abby let out a surprised laugh. "That's the understatement of the century. I'm thinking complete gut job here."

"Probably wise. Though, that tub could be restored if you wanted to keep a vintage element. They're actually quite sought after, and the quality is excellent."

Abby considered this, tilting her head thoughtfully. "I hadn't thought of that. It would add character while still allowing for modern updates elsewhere."

"Exactly. A bridge between old and new." Mike made a note on his clipboard. "We'd need to reinforce the floor if we keep it, though. These old cast iron tubs are extremely heavy."

"Noted. Let's head up to the attic. The third floor is mostly the same. It was rarely ever used. Those rooms are all empty and really just need cleaned, fresh paint and some updated lighting."

The attic stairs creaked ominously as they climbed, and Mike instinctively offered his hand to Abby when a step shifted slightly beneath her foot. She hesitated for just a moment before accepting it, her fingers cool and slender against his calloused palm. The contact lasted only seconds before she stepped onto the more solid attic floor, but the brief touch sent an unexpected jolt through him.

"These stairs would definitely need reinforcing," he said, clearing his throat and focusing on the task at hand.

The attic was spacious but dim, with small dormer windows providing limited light. Dust motes danced in the air, and the space was filled with boxes, old furniture, and various forgotten items draped in sheets.

"I haven't even begun to sort through all this," Abby admitted, gesturing to the cluttered space. "It's a bit overwhelming."

"It's a lot," Mike agreed. "But the structure itself looks solid."

He walked across the floor, testing for weak spots, while Abby remained near the stairs, watching him with an expression he couldn't quite read.

"What are your thoughts on converting this to livable space?" she asked. "Would that add significant value?"

Mike considered the question, looking around at the potential. "It could, depending on how it's done. You've got enough square footage up here for a nice bonus room or even a master suite. The ceiling height is decent in the center, though you'd lose some space along the eaves."

"What about egress requirements for a bedroom?"

"We'd need to add proper windows or dormers for code compliance. It's doable, but not inexpensive."

"Let's put that in the 'maybe' column for now. I'd rather focus on updating the existing rooms if we're trying to stay within the three-month timeline."

"That's a reasonable approach," Mike agreed. "Especially since you're working with a fixed timeline."

They made their way back downstairs and finally to the basement, a cavernous space with stone foundation walls, a concrete floor, and exposed ceiling joists. The air was cool and damp, with the faint musty smell common to old basements.

"Not much to do down here except address any moisture issues," Mike said, shining his flashlight along the foundation walls. "I'm seeing some efflorescence on these stones, which indicates water infiltration."

"Is that serious?" Abby asked, stepping closer to examine where he had pointed.

"It can be if left untreated. Water is a house's worst enemy. I'd recommend improving the drainage around the foundation and possibly applying a waterproofing solution to these walls."

"Expensive?"

"It depends on how extensive the problem is. I'd want to check the gutters and downspouts too. Often the issue starts with improper water diversion from the roof."

Abby made a note on her tablet, her brow furrowed in concentration. "I keep thinking I'm getting a handle on the scope of this project, and then another issue pops up."

"That's pretty standard with older homes," Mike said gently. "They tend to reveal their secrets slowly. But the good news is, nothing I've seen so far is a deal-breaker. The structure is fundamentally sound, which is the most important thing."

She looked up at him, seeming to study his face. "You're really knowledgeable about all this."

Mike felt a flush of pleasure at her approval. "I've been working on old houses since I was a teenager. My dad was in construction too, taught me everything he knew. Then I studied architectural design for a couple of years before deciding I preferred the hands-on work."

"Why did you switch?" Abby asked, surprising him with her interest.

Mike considered how to answer. "I guess I realized I enjoy the tangible aspects of building more than just designing on paper. I like seeing immediate results, solving problems in real-time, working with my hands." He smiled slightly. "Plus, I wasn't much for sitting at a desk all day."

Abby nodded, a flicker of understanding in her eyes. "I can respect that. Though I obviously went the other direction, design school, then working my way up the corporate ladder until..."

"Until you could partner at Reed Interiors," Mike finished when she trailed off.

"Right." Her expression closed slightly. "Well, shall we head back upstairs to discuss the next steps?"

They returned to the kitchen, where Abby refilled their coffee mugs with warm coffee before spreading her preliminary plans across the table. Mike was impressed with her thoroughness. She'd created detailed layouts for each room, complete with material specifications and design notes.

"These are excellent," he said, genuinely impressed. "You've clearly thought through the functional aspects as well as the aesthetics."

"That's my job," she replied, but he could tell she appreciated the compliment. "The question is, how much of this is feasible within the timeframe and budget?"

Mike rubbed his jaw thoughtfully. "That's the million-dollar question, isn't it? Let me break it down by priority."

For the next hour, they worked side by side, heads bent over the plans as Mike outlined what he saw as essential improvements versus optional upgrades. Their hands occasionally brushed as they pointed to different areas of the drawings, and Mike couldn't help noticing how perfectly they seemed to fit into the rhythm of collaboration together. Her asking precise questions, him offering practical solutions.

"If we focus on the kitchen, bathrooms, and critical systems, plumbing, electrical, and HVAC, that leaves cosmetic updates for the rest of the house," Mike summarized. "Paint, refinished floors, updated light fixtures. Those things will make a huge visual impact without breaking the bank."

Abby nodded, making notes. "What about the exterior? The paint is peeling badly, and the porch has several rotted boards."

"That should definitely be addressed. Curb appeal is crucial for selling, and those rotted boards are a safety issue. I'd also recommend having the roof inspected, even though it looks okay from what I could see."

"So, what's your ballpark estimate?" Abby asked, looking up at him with those direct hazel eyes.

Mike took a deep breath. This was always the moment of truth with clients. "Based on what I've seen today and the scope we've discussed, I'd estimate between $85,000 and $110,000, depending on final material selections and any surprises we might uncover once we start opening walls."

Abby didn't flinch. "That's... actually lower than I expected. The last contractor I spoke with in Charleston quoted nearly twice that for a similar scope."

"Charleston, South Carolina prices are different from Laurel Ridge prices," Mike explained. "Lower overhead, different labor rates. Plus, I try to keep my pricing fair. I'd rather build a reputation for quality work at reasonable rates than maximize profit on each job."

"That's refreshing. In Charleston, I've dealt with plenty of contractors who seemed more interested in their bottom line than the actual work."

"That's not how we do things at Hatfield House Doctors," Mike said simply. "I can get you a detailed estimate in a day or so if that works?"

"Perfect." Abby gathered her papers. "And your timeline? Do you think three months is feasible?"

Mike considered this carefully. "It's tight but doable if we don't hit any major surprises and if the material selections are finalized quickly. I'd want to start within the next few days to stay on track."

"I can work with that. I'll need to be heavily involved in the design decisions, of course."

"I wouldn't have it any other way," Mike assured her. "It's your vision, after all. We're just here to implement it."

"Good. Then I think we have an understanding."

They walked toward the front door, the inspection complete. On the porch, Mike paused, turning to face her.

"One more thing," he said. "Would you be open to documenting the renovation process? Before and after photos, maybe some progress shots? With a historic property like this, it could make for a great portfolio piece for both of us."

Abby considered this. "That's actually a good idea. It could be useful marketing material when I launch my firm."

"Exactly. Plus, you'd be preserving a bit of your family's legacy."

Something flickered in her eyes at that. "I hadn't thought of it that way, but yes, I suppose that's true."

An awkward silence fell between them, neither quite sure how to conclude their meeting. Finally, Mike extended his hand.

"It was a pleasure working with you today, Ms. Marshall. I look forward to your decision once you've reviewed my estimate."

"Abby," she corrected, taking his hand.

Her hand felt small but strong in his, and Mike allowed himself a genuine smile. "Abby, then. And I'm Mike, not Mr. Hatfield."

"Mike," she repeated, as if testing the name. A small smile curved her lips. "I'll be waiting for your estimate."

As Mike drove away, he couldn't help feeling a sense of anticipation. The project itself was exciting, a chance to restore a significant piece of Laurel Ridge history, but he knew his enthusiasm went beyond professional interest.

There was something about Abby that had always intrigued him. Not just her beauty, though she was certainly beautiful, but her determination, her precise mind, the flashes of vulnerability she tried so hard to conceal. Working with her would be challenging, rewarding, and probably complicated.

Six months, he reminded himself. She'd be in Laurel Ridge for at least six months, and then she'd return to Charleston, back to her real life. His job was to help her achieve her goal, not complicate it with unwanted attention.

With that sobering thought, Mike turned his truck toward his office, already mentally drafting the detailed estimate that needed to be nothing short of perfect.

Chapter 6

Abby stood on the porch long after Mike's truck disappeared down the driveway, processing their meeting. She hadn't expected to be so... impressed. Mike Hatfield clearly knew his business. His assessment had been thorough, his suggestions practical, and his pricing surprisingly reasonable.

More than that, there was something reassuring about his presence, a steadiness, and competence that put her at ease despite the daunting project ahead. He listened when she spoke, really listened, considering her ideas with respect rather than the condescension she'd sometimes encountered from male contractors in Charleston.

Returning to the kitchen, Abby gathered her papers and organized them into neat piles. The morning's walkthrough had been productive, clarifying both the scope of work and the approach they would take. It had also confirmed what she'd already suspected: Mike was the right contractor for this job.

So why did that realization make her feel so unsettled?

Perhaps it was the way his eyes crinkled when he smiled, or how carefully he'd offered his hand on those creaky attic stairs, or the knowledge that he'd known her in high school. The idea that he might remember that awkward, insecure version of herself made her uncomfortable, as if her carefully constructed professional persona might somehow be transparent to him.

Abby shook her head, dismissing these thoughts. This was business, nothing more. Getting distracted by a contractor, no matter how competent or kind, wasn't part of the plan.

Her phone buzzed with a text from Leslie: Dinner still on for tonight? Dying to hear how it went with Mike!

Abby typed a quick reply: Yes, to dinner. The inspection went well. Professional and thorough.

Leslie's response was immediate: Boooring. I want details! 6pm, my place.

Smiling, Abby set down her phone. Leslie hadn't changed since high school, still enthusiastic, still nosy, and still determined to find romance everywhere she looked. It was endearing, if occasionally exhausting.

Glancing around the kitchen, Abby felt the weight of the project ahead, the decisions to be made, the budget to manage, the timeline to maintain. But mixed with that weight was a surprising flicker of excitement. For all its challenges, this renovation represented an opportunity to prove herself to the people of Laurel Ridge, to create something beautiful and valuable from what had been neglected.

And working with Mike might not be as tedious as she'd initially feared. In fact, if this morning was any indication, it might even be... pleasant.

"Focus, Abby," she murmured to herself, gathering her tablet and heading toward the study. She had material selections to research and budgets to refine before dinner with Leslie.

The renovation was the priority. Everything else, including unexpected thoughts about a certain contractor's warm hazel eyes, was just a distraction.

***

"So, let me get this straight," Leslie said. "You spent four hours with the most eligible bachelor in Laurel Ridge, and all you have to say is that he's 'competent' and 'thorough'?"

They were sitting on Leslie's patio, enjoying the mild spring evening. Leslie's apartment was above her flower shop, with a small but charming outdoor space filled with potted plants and twinkling string lights. The remains of their dinner, a delicious homemade pasta, sat forgotten on the table between them.

"What else would I say about my contractor?"

"Oh, I don't know." Leslie's eyes sparkled mischievously. "Maybe that he's got shoulders like a lumberjack? Or that he's the kind of guy who probably rescues kittens from trees in his spare time?"

Abby couldn't help laughing. "Has he actually rescued kittens from trees?"

"Mrs. Lawson's cat last summer. Climbed right up that big oak tree by the library without hesitation." Leslie leaned forward. "But you're deflecting. Did you at least notice he's handsome?"

"I'm not blind, Leslie. Yes, he's attractive, in a rugged, mountain-man sort of way."

"Progress!" Leslie clinked her water glass against Abby's. "Now we're getting somewhere."

Abby rolled her eyes. "We're not getting anywhere. I'm hiring him to renovate the house, not date him."

"Who says you can't do both?"

"Professional ethics? Common sense? The fact that I'm leaving in six months, less if the house sells quickly?"

Leslie waved these objections away. "Details, details. The point is, you're a beautiful, successful, single woman, and he's a handsome, single, and successful man. In a small town. Working together daily. It's practically a romance movie waiting to happen."

"My life is not a romance movie. It's a carefully planned career strategy that hit a temporary setback. Charleston is where I belong, not here."

Leslie's expression softened. "Is it, though? You never seemed particularly happy when you visited from Charleston in the past. Stressed, for sure. Busy, most definitely. But happy? I'm not so sure."

Abby felt a flicker of defensiveness. "I was building something important. That takes sacrifice."

"I know," Leslie said. "And you're incredibly talented. I just wonder sometimes if you're running toward something or away from something."

The question hit uncomfortably close to home, and Abby changed the subject. "Tell me about your business. The shop looked busy when I walked by yesterday."

Leslie allowed the redirect with grace. "It's going really well. Wedding season is ramping up, and I've got three big events next month. Plus the usual daily orders."

"That's wonderful. I'm not surprised you're successful. You always had a way with anything that was green, and growing things, even in high school."

"Remember when I convinced Mr. Peterson to let us grow vegetables in that strip of land behind the science building?" Leslie laughed. "You designed the layout."

"And you kept everything alive," Abby smiled at the memory. "We made a good team."

"We still could," Leslie said casually, too casually. "You know, if you decided to stay."

Abby shook her head. "Don't start. My plan is set."

"Plans change," Leslie shrugged. "Just saying."

They sat in comfortable silence for a moment, the evening breeze carrying the scent of Leslie's potted jasmine.

"Did you know," Leslie said eventually, refilling their glasses, "that Mike had a massive crush on you in high school?"

Abby nearly choked on her water. "What? No, he didn't."

"Oh, yes, he did. He was just too shy to do anything about it. He used to watch you in the library when you were studying."

"That sounds more creepy than romantic."

"It wasn't like that," Leslie insisted. "He was just... admiring from afar. He told Tyler's mom, his late wife, Cora, about it once, and she shared it with me. She thought it was sweet."

"I didn't realize he had a wife who passed away. That's awful."

"Yes, during childbirth with Tyler. It was really tragic. Mike was devastated. He doesn't talk about Cora's death much," Leslie explained. "But everyone in town knows the story. He's raised Tyler on his own, and built his business from scratch while being a single dad. That's why all the single women in Laurel Ridge have had their eye on him for years... well, that and because he's so handsome and kind. He's one of the good guys."

"Yet he remains single," Abby observed.

"He's picky. And busy. And probably a little gun-shy after losing Cora." Leslie gave her a meaningful look. "But he did have a soft spot for you at one time, that much I know."

"That was a teenage crush, if it even existed. We're adults now, with complicated lives and responsibilities."

"All the more reason to find happiness where you can," Leslie said, suddenly serious. "Life's too short for anything else. If there's one thing this town has learned from seeing what Mike went through, it's that."

"I get what you're trying to do, Leslie, but please stop. I'm not looking for a relationship, especially not one with a built-in expiration date."

Leslie raised her hands in surrender. "Fine, fine. But don't be surprised if the universe has other plans. Your aunt Gertrude always said God works in mysterious ways."

"She also said not to eat dessert before dinner, but that never stopped you," Abby countered, deliberately lightening the mood.

Leslie laughed. "True! Speaking of which, I have chocolate mousse in the fridge. Want some?"

"Absolutely."

As Leslie went inside to get dessert, Abby leaned back in her chair, looking up at the stars emerging in the darkening sky. They were so much brighter here than in Charleston, where the city lights dimmed their brilliance.

Despite her protests to Leslie, the revelation about Mike's teenage crush lingered in her mind. It was strange to think of him watching her all those years ago, seeing something in her that had caught his attention.

Leslie returned with two dishes of chocolate mousse. "Here you go. Guaranteed to solve all of life's problems for at least ten minutes."

Abby smiled gratefully, both for the dessert and for Leslie's friendship. "Thanks. For everything."

"That's what friends are for," Leslie said simply. "That, and telling you when a hot contractor is secretly in love with you."

"He is not in love with me!"

"Yet," Leslie winked. "Just wait until you start picking out bathroom fixtures together. Very romantic."

Chapter 7

Abby flipped through Mike's detailed renovation proposal, impressed. The thirteen-page document outlined everything they'd discussed during the walkthrough, complete with timeline projections, material allowances, and payment schedules. He'd even included photographs of the problem areas they'd identified, each annotated with proposed solutions.

"This is..." She searched for a word that wouldn't sound overly complimentary. "Comprehensive."

Mike nodded from behind his desk. "I try to be thorough. Helps avoid surprises down the road."

Abby turned to the budget breakdown, running her finger down the columns of figures. The total came to $103,450... on the higher end of his initial estimate, but still reasonable given the scope of work. And, notably, almost half of what she would have paid in Charleston for comparable quality.

"Some of these allowances might be adjusted depending on your final selections," Mike explained, leaning forward slightly. "The kitchen and bathroom fixtures, for instance. If you choose higher-end items than what I've budgeted for, we'd need to account for that difference."

"Of course, and these contingency funds?"

"Standard practice for old homes. Ten percent of the total budget set aside for unexpected issues." He tapped the paper with his pen. "If we don't need it, you don't pay it."

She glanced up, meeting his eyes. "That's fair."

The office felt different today than during her first visit. Sunlight streamed through the windows, highlighting the organized clutter of blueprints and material samples. A child's drawing was pinned to the bulletin board behind Mike's desk.

"Any other questions about the proposal?" Mike asked, his voice pulling her attention back to the task at hand.

"Are you confident you can complete everything in three months?"

"Barring major surprises, yes. I've can schedule additional crew members for critical phases, and we can work weekends if needed to stay on track."

"That would be appreciated." She hesitated, then added, "I should mention I plan to live in the house during the renovation. Will that be a problem?"

"It'll be dusty and noisy, especially during demolition. And you'd be without a working kitchen for at least two weeks."

"I've survived worse," Abby said dryly.

"We typically rope off work areas with plastic sheeting to contain the dust, but it still manages to get everywhere." He studied her expression. "If you're determined to stay, we'll do our best to minimize the disruption."

"I appreciate that." Abby returned to the proposal, turning to the payment schedule. "These progressive payments work for me. Thirty percent deposit is standard."

Mike pulled a contract from his desk drawer. "I've drawn up the formal agreement based on our discussions. Take your time reviewing it. If everything looks good, we can sign today and get started on Monday."

Abby accepted the document, skimming through the legal language. It mirrored the proposal terms, clearly outlining responsibilities, timelines, and payment structures. Everything appeared straightforward and reasonable.

She'd come prepared to negotiate, to push back on points that seemed excessive or unwarranted. But there was nothing to object to. Mike was either refreshingly honest or the shrewdest businessman she'd encountered in years.

"This all looks acceptable," she said, reaching for her pen. "I have one addition, though."

Mike raised a questioning eyebrow.

"I'd like to include a provision about my involvement in the design process. I need to approve all finishes, fixtures, and color selections before installation." She met his gaze directly. "It's important that the renovation reflects my vision as a designer."

"Absolutely," Mike agreed without hesitation. "I wouldn't have it any other way. This is your project. We're just the hands making it happen." He pulled the contract back, adding a handwritten clause at the bottom of the second page. "How's this? 'All design elements, including but not limited to fixtures, finishes, colors, and hardware, are subject to client approval prior to purchase or installation.'"

Abby nodded, surprised and pleased by his immediate accommodation. "Perfect."

Mike added a line, initialed it, then slid the contract back across the desk. Abby signed her name at the bottom, then watched as Mike did the same. Just like that, the project was officially underway.

"I'll get a copy made for your records," Mike said, standing. He moved to the copier in the corner of the office, giving Abby a moment to observe him more carefully.

He wore another button-down shirt today, forest green that complemented his hazel eyes, sleeves rolled to reveal tanned forearms. His movements were efficient and purposeful, without the nervous energy she'd detected during their first meeting. This was Mike in his element, confident, competent, and at ease in his professional domain.

He returned with her copy of the contract, which she tucked into her leather portfolio. "That should do it. I'll get the deposit check to you this afternoon."

"Perfect." Mike hesitated, then added, "I was thinking we should go over some of the material choices soon. Maybe get a head start on selections that have longer lead times."

"Good idea. I can put together some design boards this weekend."

"Great." Mike glanced at his watch. "It's almost eleven. Would you like to grab coffee? To celebrate finalizing the contract?" He quickly added, "We could walk through some preliminary ideas for the kitchen and bathrooms."

Abby paused, momentarily caught off guard by the invitation. It sounded innocent enough, a business discussion over coffee, nothing more. And yet something in his expression, a flicker of uncertainty, suggested the invitation had taken some courage.

Leslie's voice echoed in her mind: Mike Hatfield had a massive crush on you in high school.

"Coffee would be fine," she said. "Martha's?"

"Perfect," Mike agreed, visibly relaxing. "It's usually quieter this time of day, between the breakfast and lunch rushes."

They gathered their things and headed out, walking side by side down the sunny main street. The mid-morning air was fresh and cool, carrying the scent of spring blossoms from planters lining the sidewalk.

"I've been thinking about the upstairs bathroom," Abby said. "You mentioned keeping the claw-foot tub. I'm leaning toward that option. It has character that would appeal to buyers."

"It's a beautiful piece," Mike agreed. "Needs some refinishing, but that's straightforward. We could pair it with more modern fixtures for the sink and toilet to balance the vintage element."

"Exactly what I was thinking. Clean white subway tile on the walls, maybe a marble-topped vanity." She found herself warming to the topic. "The floor is where I'm torn. Period-appropriate hexagon tiles would be authentic, but a wood-look porcelain might be more practical."

"The hexagon tiles would make a statement," Mike offered. "But you're right about practicality. The wood-look is more forgiving and lower maintenance."

They reached the diner, Mike holding the door open for her. As Mike had predicted, the diner was quiet, with only a few tables occupied. There were a couple of older men in a corner booth, a woman typing on her laptop near the windows, and a mother with a toddler at a table near the back.

Martha looked up from behind the counter, her face brightening. "Well, look who it is! Abby and Mike... now there's a sight that does my heart good."

Abby felt a flush creep up her neck. "We're discussing renovation plans, Martha. Mike's handling the project for Aunt Gertrude's house."

"Sure, sure," Martha nodded, her eyes twinkling. "Business meeting. Very official. Coffee for both of you?"

"Please," Mike said, gesturing toward a booth by the window. "We'll take that table, if that's alright."

"Make yourselves comfortable," Martha called, already reaching for the coffee pot. "I just pulled a fresh apple pie from the oven if you're interested."

The booth's red vinyl seats squeaked as they slid in opposite each other. Sunlight streamed through the large window, highlighting the Formica tabletop. Abby removed her portfolio from her bag, arranging it neatly before her.

"Martha's pies are legendary," Mike said. "Seems a shame to skip it when we're celebrating a new project."

"Is that what we're doing? Celebrating?" Abby asked, one eyebrow raised.

Mike's cheeks colored slightly. "Well, signing a contract is a milestone worth marking, don't you think? Even if it's just with coffee and pie."

Martha appeared with two steaming mugs and a slice of pie with two forks. "The pies on the house," she declared, setting it between them. "I always like to see new partnerships start off sweet."

"Thank you, Martha," Abby said politely. "But we're just—"

"Working together. I get it, honey." Martha winked at Mike. "You two enjoy. Holler if you need anything else."

As Martha retreated to the counter, Abby turned her attention to her coffee, adding a splash of cream from the small metal pitcher on the table. She was acutely aware of Mike watching her, his expression thoughtful.

"You mentioned design boards for the weekend," he said, redirecting the conversation to safer territory. "Any preliminary thoughts on the kitchen style?"

Abby nodded, grateful for the professional focus. "I'm thinking clean, classic lines. White shaker cabinets, subway tile back splash, possibly butcher block on the island with quartz countertops elsewhere." She took a sip of her coffee. "It needs to be timeless, but with enough character to feel special."

"That sounds perfect for the house," Mike agreed. "Would you be open to some industrial-style pendant lights over the island? I've seen those paired with traditional elements to create a nice balance in historic homes."

"I could see that working," Abby said, genuinely impressed by his suggestion. "Maybe in a brushed brass finish to warm up the space."

"Exactly." Mike's face lit up with enthusiasm. "And speaking of warmth, what if we incorporated some reclaimed wood elements? I have access to some beautiful old barn beams that could be repurposed as floating shelves or even a decorative beam across the ceiling."

Abby found herself smiling at his excitement. "I like your style, Mike. Those are excellent suggestions."

He ducked his head slightly, looking almost bashful at the compliment. "Just ideas. You're the design expert."

"True, but you clearly understand how to respect a home's character while updating it for modern living." She hesitated, then added, "That's not as common as you might think. Many contractors just want to tear everything out and start fresh."

"That approach has its place, but not in a home like yours. There's too much history there to disregard."

Abby nodded. She picked up her fork and took a small bite of the pie, which was indeed exceptional, tart apples, perfectly balanced sweetness, and a flaky crust that practically melted on her tongue.

"Martha wasn't exaggerating about the pie," she said. "It's delicious."

Mike took a bite as well, nodding in agreement. "She claims the secret is lard in the crust, but she won't confirm or deny."

"Some secrets are worth keeping, I suppose."

"Speaking of which," Mike said carefully, "would you mind if I asked you something about your design career? Please don't hesitate to say no if it's too personal."

Abby tensed slightly, but maintained her composure. "What would you like to know?"

"What drew you to interior design? Was it something you always wanted to do, or did you discover it later?"

The question surprised her, not intrusive or overly personal, but genuinely curious. "I suppose it started here, actually," she found herself admitting. "Living with Aunt Gertrude and Uncle Wilburn, I was surrounded by beautiful architecture and thoughtful design. Uncle Wilburn's work, especially the way he considered how spaces would be used, how light would fall throughout the day."

Mike nodded encouragingly, his expression open and interested.

"When I went to college, I initially thought I'd follow in his footsteps with architecture," Abby continued. "But I discovered I was more drawn to the interior elements, how spaces feel, how they function, how people interact with them." She traced a pattern on the tabletop with her finger. "There's something powerful about creating environments that shape people's daily experiences, you know?"

"I do know," Mike said. "It's why I love renovation work. People spend so much of their lives inside their homes, they should be places that bring comfort and joy, not frustration."

Their eyes met across the table, and for a moment, Abby felt a spark of connection, the shared understanding of people who valued the same things, spoke the same language of spaces and materials and purpose.

"What about you?" she asked, surprising herself with her interest. "How did you get into renovation?"

Mike took a sip of his coffee before answering. "My dad was a carpenter. I grew up tagging along on job sites, learning how to use tools before I could ride a bike. But renovation specifically?" He considered the question. "I love the problem-solving aspect of it. Each old house has its quirks and challenges. There's something satisfying about figuring out how to honor what's there while making it work for modern life."

"That makes sense. It's like a puzzle."

"Exactly. A three-dimensional puzzle that sometimes fights back with hidden water damage and knob-and-tube wiring."

Abby laughed, a genuine, unguarded sound. His eyes crinkled at the corners when he smiled in response.

"So Hatfield House Doctors," she said. "Tell me about that. Was it always the plan to start your own company?"

Mike shook his head. "Not initially. I worked for Bennett Construction after college. Good company, solid training ground. But after..." He hesitated briefly. "After Tyler was born, I needed more flexibility. Being my own boss meant I could schedule work around his needs."

Abby noted the pause, remembering what Leslie had told her about Mike's wife dying in childbirth. She wondered if she should acknowledge it or let it pass unremarked.

"That sounds challenging," she said carefully. "Building a business while raising a child."

"It was, and it still is," Mike admitted. "But worth it. Tyler's a great kid. He makes it all worthwhile." His expression softened when he mentioned his son. "Plus, I get to choose projects I believe in. Like yours."

"Lucky me," Abby said lightly, deflecting the compliment.

"Lucky us," Mike countered. "The Marshall home is a significant piece of Laurel Ridge history. Being part of its restoration is meaningful work."

His sincerity was disarming, making it difficult for Abby to maintain her professional detachment. She found herself wondering what it would be like to work with someone who approached projects with such genuine care and appreciation.

"Martha mentioned you've been coming here since you were a kid," Mike said, changing the subject. "Any other favorite spots in Laurel Ridge?"

Abby considered the question. "The library. Uncle Wilburn designed it, so I might be biased, but I always loved the reading room there. And then the path along Anderson Creek, Aunt Gertrude and I used to walk there on Sunday afternoons."

"The creek trail is one of Tyler's favorites too," Mike said. "There's a perfect climbing tree about halfway down that he's determined to conquer."

"The old oak with the low branches?" Abby smiled at the memory. "I used to climb that tree myself. There's a perfect spot near the top where you can see all the way to Miller's Farm."

"That's the one." Mike looked pleased by this shared knowledge. "Tyler's only made it to the middle branches so far, but he's nothing if not persistent."

"A good quality to have."

Their conversation flowed easily for the next half hour, touching on Laurel Ridge landmarks, renovation challenges, and design trends. Abby found herself relaxing, drawn into Mike's thoughtful observations and quiet humor. When she mentioned her plans for the living room built-ins, he offered suggestions for refinishing techniques that would preserve their character while refreshing their appearance.

"You really care about the details," she noted, impressed by his knowledge of wood restoration.

"The details are what make a house special," Mike replied. "Anyone can gut a room and make it functional. But respecting the crafts-manship that went into these older homes? That takes patience and attention."

Abby nodded, feeling a new appreciation for his approach. "Well, I'm glad to have someone on the project who understands that."

Mike glanced at his watch and straightened. "I should probably get back to the office. I've got a client meeting at one."

"Of course," Abby gathered her portfolio, suddenly aware they'd spent nearly an hour talking. "I've taken up too much of your morn-ing."

"Not at all," Mike assured her. "This was... helpful."

Abby nodded, accepting his framing of their conversation as pure-ly professional, though it had wandered well beyond construction specifics.

They stood, both reaching for the check Martha had left on the table. Their hands brushed briefly, and Abby withdrew hers, feeling oddly flustered.

"Please, let me," Mike said. "Like I said, we're celebrating a new project."

"At least let me leave the tip," Abby insisted, already reaching for her wallet.

Mike acquiesced with a smile. "Fair enough."

After they left the diner, they paused on the sidewalk. Abby was suddenly unsure of the proper goodbye protocol for what had begun as a business meeting but had evolved into something more personal.

"I'll stop by the bank this afternoon and drop off the deposit check," she said, retreating to the safety of business details.

"Perfect. And I'll start ordering materials. We should be able to begin demolition on Monday, if that works for you."

"Monday is fine. Earlier is better, actually. I'm eager to get started."

Mike nodded. "One more thing. Do you have plans for Sunday morning? The reason I ask is if you're interested, Laurel Ridge Community Church has a service at ten. Pastor Whitman is excellent, and it might be a good way to reconnect with the community while you're in town."

The invitation caught Abby off guard. She hadn't attended church regularly in Charleston, though she'd grown up going with Aunt Gertrude every Sunday. Something about Mike's suggestion stirred a long-dormant sense of longing, not just for community, but for the peace she'd once found in those quiet Sunday mornings.

"Maybe," she said.

"You probably remember Pastor Thompson. He's retired now," Mike explained. "Andrew Whitman took over last year. Young guy, but thoughtful. Down-to-earth."

"I'll give it a try," Abby decided. "It would be nice to see how the church has changed."

Mike's expression brightened. "Great. I'll see you there. Tyler and I usually sit about halfway back, left side."

They said their goodbyes, Mike heading back toward his office while Abby turned in the direction of the Victorian. As she walked, she replayed their conversation, surprised by how easily they'd connected once they moved beyond strictly professional topics.

It's just coffee, she reminded herself. *A business meeting with pie.*

Yet, she couldn't quite dismiss the warm feeling that had settled in her chest. A sense of connection she hadn't experienced in a long time.

Charleston, for all its sophistication and opportunities, had often felt lonely. Her colleagues at Reed Interiors had been competitive at worst, cordially professional at best. None had shown the genuine interest or easy camaraderie she'd just experienced over coffee with Mike.

Don't read too much into it, she cautioned herself. *He's being friendly because you're a client, an important one for a small-town business.*

Still, as she walked up the winding path to the Victorian's front porch, she found herself looking forward to Sunday morning in a way that surprised her. The prospect of sitting in those familiar pews, hearing the old hymns, feeling part of something larger than herself, it called to a part of her soul that had been neglected in the rush of building her career.

Inside the house, she settled at the kitchen table with her laptop, intending to work. Instead, she opened a browser and searched for "Laurel Ridge Community Church." The website was simple but well-designed, featuring a message from Pastor Whitman about faith, community, and finding a home in unexpected places.

Abby read his welcome message twice, something in his words resonating with her current situation:

"Whether you're a lifelong resident or just passing through, know that you are welcome here. Faith isn't about perfection, it's about connection. Connection to God, to each other, and to the purpose He has for each of us. Sometimes that purpose reveals itself in unexpected ways and places. Our job isn't to question the journey, but to remain open to where it leads."

She closed the browser, unsettled by how the message seemed to speak directly to her circumstance. Was returning to Laurel Ridge part of some larger purpose? The practical, career-focused part of her scoffed at the notion. This was a business decision, nothing more, a strategic retreat to rebuild her resources before returning to her real life in Charleston.

And yet, today's conversation with Mike had stirred something in her, a whisper of possibility, a question about what "real life" truly meant. In Charleston, she'd achieved the external markers of success: prestigious clients, professional recognition, and a stylish apartment in a desirable neighborhood. But had she found genuine connection? Purpose beyond the next project, the next promotion?

Abby shook her head, dismissing these unsettling thoughts. She had a plan, one she'd carefully crafted after the disaster at Reed Interiors. Questioning that plan based on coffee and pie with an attractive contractor was ridiculous.

Focus, Abby, she told herself firmly. *Design boards. Material selections. Timeline management. These are the priorities.*

Yet as she opened her design software and began creating concept boards for the kitchen renovation, her mind kept drifting to the invitation for Sunday, to the possibility of connecting with something beyond her career ambitions. Something she hadn't even realized she'd been missing until today.

Maybe Leslie's right, a small voice whispered in the back of her mind. *Maybe there is more to find in Laurel Ridge than just a renovated house to sell.*

For once, Abby didn't immediately silence the thought. Instead, she let it linger as she worked, a quiet counterpoint to the practical considerations of cabinet styles and counter materials. And if her design choices began to reflect not just what would appeal to future buyers, but what might make the house feel like a true home again—well, that was simply good design sense, wasn't it?

Chapter 8

Abby sat in her car outside Laurel Ridge Community Church, fingers tapping nervously on the steering wheel. The white clapboard building with its elegant steeple looked exactly as it had during her childhood, timeless against the backdrop of the Appalachian mountains. The parking lot was filling quickly as families arrived for the ten o'clock service.

She'd spent too much time deliberating over her outfit this morning, finally settling on a simple blue dress that struck the right balance between respectful and casual. Now she was questioning everything, from her choice of shoes to her decision to come at all.

"This is ridiculous," she muttered, reaching for her purse. "It's just church."

But it wasn't just church. It was her first public appearance in the Laurel Ridge community beyond Martha's Diner. It meant facing people who might remember her as "that poor Marshall girl" whose parents had abandoned her. People who would assess how she'd turned out, judge whether she'd overcome her troubled beginnings, or whisper about her return.

The church bell began to toll, its clear, resonant sound cutting through her hesitation. Ten chimes. Service was starting.

With a deep breath, Abby opened her car door and stepped out. She smoothed her dress, straightened her shoulders, and walked toward the church entrance.

As she approached the double doors, a middle-aged couple smiled at her. "Good morning," the woman said. "Beautiful day for worship."

"Yes, it is," Abby replied.

Inside, the church was just as she remembered: polished wooden pews, stained-glass windows casting jewel-toned light across the sanctuary floor, a simple wooden cross at the altar. Yet, there were subtle changes too: updated hymnals, a new sound system, a projection screen that could be lowered from the ceiling. Tradition meeting modern needs.

The sanctuary was nearly full, conversations creating a gentle hum throughout the space. Abby hesitated in the back, scanning for an inconspicuous seat, preferably toward the rear where fewer people would notice her.

"Abby? Abby Marshall?"

She turned to find Emma Talbot waving from a pew about halfway down the left side. The blonde was beaming, beckoning Abby to join her.

Emma Talbot. They'd been friendly in high school, though not as close as she and Leslie. Emma had always been unfailingly kind, organizing care packages when Abby had mono her junior year, and inviting her to study groups even when Abby usually declined.

Mike's words echoed in her mind: *Tyler and I usually sit about halfway back, left side.*

Her pulse quickened. She scanned the pew and spotted him a few seats down, his head bent toward a small boy with dark, tousled hair. He was pointing to something in a children's Bible, his expression gentle and focused.

Part of her wanted to find another seat, but Emma was still waving, now drawing attention from nearby congregants. Hiding wasn't an option.

With a small smile, Abby made her way to Emma's pew, sliding in beside her.

"I can't believe it's really you," Emma whispered, giving Abby's arm a quick squeeze. "Leslie mentioned you were back, but I wasn't sure if you'd be at church. It's so good to see you!"

"It's good to see you too," Abby replied, surprised to find she meant it. "You haven't changed a bit."

Emma laughed softly. "Oh, I've changed plenty. I run the General Store now, took over from my parents five years ago."

"That's wonderful. I loved that store as a kid."

"You'll have to come by. I still keep those caramel candies you used to like near the register." Emma's easy recall of this detail touched Abby unexpectedly.

Down the pew, Mike had noticed her arrival. He offered a warm smile that made something flutter in Abby's chest. Tyler looked up too, tilting his head curiously before offering a shy smile.

Abby smiled back, relieved when the organ began to play, signaling the start of the service. She reached for a hymnal as the congregation rose, and Abby found herself singing words she hadn't uttered in years but still knew by heart.

"Great is Thy faithfulness, O God my Father, There is no shadow of turning with Thee; Thou changest not, Thy compassions, they fail not; As Thou hast been Thou forever wilt be."

The music filled the sanctuary, voices raised in harmony. Abby felt a tightness in her throat, a prickling behind her eyes. There was something powerful about these words, and this communal act of worship that transcended time and circumstance. For a moment, she could almost feel Aunt Gertrude beside her, singing in her clear, confident soprano. This had been her favorite song.

As the congregation settled back into their seats, a young man stepped up to the pulpit. He appeared to be in his mid-thirties, with an open, friendly face and an unassuming presence.

"Pastor Whitman?" Abby whispered to Emma.

Emma nodded. "He's been here for about a year. He's wonderful with the kids' bible study group, and his Sunday sermons actually make you think instead of lulling you to sleep."

Pastor Whitman welcomed the congregation with a warm smile, making a few announcements about upcoming events before introducing his sermon topic: "Finding Your Place: Recognizing God's Purpose in Unexpected Locations."

Abby shifted uncomfortably in her seat. The title felt eerily applicable to her current situation.

"In John 14:2, Jesus tells his disciples, 'In my Father's house are many rooms,'" Pastor Whitman began. "We often think of this verse in terms of heaven, but I believe it also speaks to our earthly journey. God prepares places for us here and now. Places where we can grow, serve, and find fulfillment."

His voice was thoughtful and conversational rather than pompous or preachy. Abby listened attentively.

"Sometimes these places are undoubtedly where we expected to be," he continued. "But often, God's plans lead us to unexpected rooms... places we never imagined ourselves, or circumstances we didn't choose."

Her eyes inadvertently met Mike's further down the pew. He gave her a small smile before returning his attention to the pastor.

"The question isn't whether God has prepared a place for you... He has. The question is whether we're willing to recognize it, even when it doesn't match our desires." Pastor Whitman's gaze swept across the congregation. "Sometimes the place we're running from is exactly where we're meant to be. Sometimes, what looks like a detour is actually the main road. And sometimes coming back isn't a step backward, but a step toward what God had planned all along."

The remainder of the sermon explored examples from scripture, Joseph sold into Egypt, Ruth following Naomi to Bethlehem, and even Jesus returning to Nazareth. Each story reinforced the theme that God's purpose often revealed itself in unexpected places and through unplanned circumstances.

Abby listened with increasing discomfort. The parallels to her situation were too pointed to ignore. Was her return to Laurel Ridge really just a practical business decision, or was there something more at work? She quickly dismissed the thought. She wasn't particularly spiritual these days, and reading divine purpose into a straightforward renovation project seemed like a stretch.

As the service concluded with a final hymn and benediction, Abby braced herself for the social interaction that would follow. She had a strategy: smile politely, exchange brief pleasantries, then make a graceful exit. Twenty minutes, maximum.

Emma had other plans. "You have to meet Pastor Whitman," she insisted, looping her arm through Abby's as they moved toward the exit. "And then a bunch of us are heading to Martha's sister's place, Lily's Café, for lunch. You'll join us, right?"

"Oh, I don't want to impose," Abby hedged.

"It's not imposing. It's catching up with old friends," Emma countered. "Leslie will be there, too. Come on, when was the last time you had Sunday lunch with friends?"

The question gave Abby pause. In Charleston, Sundays had typically meant catching up on work, preparing for Monday meetings, sometimes grabbing a quick brunch with colleagues that inevitably turned into shop talk. The thought of a relaxed meal with people who weren't evaluating her professional value was surprisingly appealing.

They reached the church entrance, where Pastor Whitman was greeting congregants. He was younger than she'd expected up close, with kind eyes and an easy smile.

"Pastor Whitman, this is Abby Marshall," Emma said. "She's Gertrude Marshall's niece, just back in town to renovate the Marshall house. You may remember her. She grew up here as well."

"Abby Marshall, what a pleasure. Your aunt was a special woman." He extended his hand, his grip warm and firm.

"Thank you," Abby said. "Your sermon was... thought-provoking."

"I'm glad to hear that," he smiled. "How long will you be staying in Laurel Ridge?"

"Just until the renovation is complete and the house sells," Abby replied automatically. "About six months, give or take."

"Well, whether it's six months or longer, you're always welcome here. And if you'd like to grab coffee sometime to talk about anything... the house, your aunt, or just life in general, my door is always open."

"Thank you, Pastor. I appreciate that."

"Andrew, please. Pastor makes me sound much more dignified than I actually am. Just ask my wife. She knows all my bad jokes."

Abby smiled. "Thank you, Andrew."

As they stepped aside to allow others to greet the pastor, Abby spotted Mike and Tyler waiting near the bottom of the church steps. The boy was pointing excitedly at something in a nearby tree, tugging on his father's hand.

Emma followed Abby's gaze. "Have you met Tyler yet? He's such a sweetheart. Hey, Mike!" She waved enthusiastically, effectively eliminating any chance Abby had of avoiding the encounter.

Mike looked up, his face brightening when he saw them. He guided Tyler toward them, one hand resting gently on the boy's shoulder.

"Good morning, Emma," he greeted, then turned to Abby with a smile that made her heart skip. "Abby. Glad you could make it today."

"The sermon was excellent," Abby replied, feeling suddenly self-conscious.

"Isn't it always?" Emma interjected. "Andrew has a way of making you think he's speaking directly to you."

"Sometimes uncomfortably so," Mike agreed with a chuckle.

Tyler was looking up at Abby with undisguised curiosity, shifting from foot to foot as if containing his energy took considerable effort.

Mike noticed his son's interest. "Tyler, this is Ms. Marshall. Remember I told you about the house we're going to be working on? This is the owner."

"The lady from the pictures?" Tyler asked, tilting his head.

"Pictures?" Abby echoed, confused.

Mike's cheeks reddened slightly. "I showed him photos of the house," he explained. "So he could understand the project, and you were in a few of them."

"Is it true you have a secret room in your attic?" Tyler asked, his eyes wide with excitement.

Abby laughed, charmed by his directness. "Not that I know of, but I haven't explored every corner yet. The attic is pretty big."

"Dad says we're going to fix your house so it looks like it did when it was brand new, even though that was like five hundred years ago."

"That's the plan," Abby agreed, smiling at his enthusiasm.

"Maybe you'll find treasure in the walls," Tyler suggested. "Joey at school said his cousin found real gold coins when they knocked down an old wall in their house."

"That would certainly help with the renovation budget," Abby replied, playing along. "I'll keep an eye out for treasure chests."

Tyler beamed at her response, then tugged at his father's sleeve. "Dad, can I go say hi to Pastor Andrew? I want to tell him about my baseball game."

"Sure, buddy. Just stay where I can see you, okay?"

Tyler nodded before darting off.

"He's got endless energy," Mike explained, watching his son fondly. "And an imagination to match."

"He's wonderful," Abby said sincerely. "How old is he?"

"Just turned eight last month. Going on eighteen, if you ask him." Mike's pride was evident in his voice.

Emma, who had been watching their interaction with obvious interest, seized the moment. "Mike, we're headed to Lily's for lunch. You and Tyler should join us."

"I wouldn't want to intrude," Mike said.

"Like I told Abby, it's not intruding. It's Sunday lunch with friends," Emma insisted. "Leslie will be there, plus a few others. It'll be fun."

Mike glanced at Abby, as if gauging her reaction to this proposition.

"Sure, that sounds nice," Mike agreed, his eyes still on Abby.

Other congregants were filtering past them now, many pausing to greet Emma or Mike. Several cast curious glances at Abby, some with looks of recognition. She steeled herself for the inevitable questions or whispers, but the interactions remained surprisingly warm.

"Is that you, Abby Marshall? Welcome back, dear."
"Gertrude would be so pleased you're taking care of the house."
"We've missed seeing a light in those windows."

Each greeting was accompanied by a smile or a gentle touch on the arm, simple gestures of welcome rather than the prying she'd feared. By the time Tyler returned, breathlessly recounting his conversation with Pastor Andrew, Abby felt some of her tension easing.

"Lily's is just down the block from Martha's place," Emma was saying. "We can walk if that works for everyone?"

They agreed, and soon their small group was strolling down Laurel Ridge's main street. The weather was perfect: warm spring sunshine tempered by a cool breeze. Tyler skipped ahead with boundless energy while the adults followed at a more measured pace.

"The church hasn't changed much," Abby observed. "Some updates, but it still feels the same."

"That's Laurel Ridge for you," Mike replied. "We embrace progress without letting go of what matters. The church got that new sound system last year, donated by the Wilson family after Mr. Wilson senior passed. They said he always complained about not being able to hear the sermons. His kids figured it was a fitting memorial."

Abby smiled at the story. "That's what I'd forgotten about small towns. Everything has a story, a connection to someone."

"It's one of the best things about living here," Mike said. "Though I suppose it can feel stifling if you're used to more anonymity."

"It's an adjustment," Abby admitted. "In Charleston, I could go weeks without running into someone I knew outside of work. Here,

I've been back less than a week and already had more personal conversations than in the last month in the city."

"Too much?" Mike asked, perceptive enough to hear the note of ambivalence in her voice.

"Different," Abby clarified. "Not bad different, just... I'm relearning the rhythms of small-town life."

Further ahead, Tyler had stopped to examine something in a storefront window, allowing Emma to catch up to him. She crouched beside him, pointing out something that made the boy laugh.

"Emma's great with kids," Mike commented. "She hosts story time at the General Store every Saturday morning. Tyler never misses it."

"She seems happy here," Abby observed. "Running the family store, involved in the community."

"She is," Mike agreed. "Emma's one of those people who knows exactly where she belongs. Never had any doubt about staying in Laurel Ridge."

"Not everyone finds their place so easily," Abby said quietly.

Mike nodded. "True enough. Sometimes it takes leaving to appreciate what you had. Sometimes leaving is exactly what you need to find something better. There's no one right way to live a life."

Chapter 9

The group arrived at Lily's Café, a cheerful corner establishment with bright yellow awnings and flower boxes bursting with colorful blooms.

Inside, the café was bustling with the post-church crowd. Checkered tablecloths covered sturdy wooden tables, and landscape paintings by local artists adorned the walls. The air was fragrant with the smell of fresh bread and roasting chicken.

A woman who bore a striking resemblance to Martha greeted them warmly. "Emma, Mike, so good to see you both." Her eyes landed on Abby with interest. "And you must be Abby Marshall. Martha told me you were back in town. I'm Lily Johnson, Martha's sister. Welcome to my café."

"It's lovely to meet you," Abby said. "Everything smells delicious."

"Sunday special is a roast chicken sandwich with all the fixings," Lily beamed. "Martha says I use too much rosemary in my chicken, but what does she know? She puts pumpkin pie spice in her apple pie."

"Which is why her pie wins at the county fair every year," Emma teased.

Lily laughed good-naturedly. "The judges have questionable taste. Come on, I've got a table ready for your group. Leslie just got here a few minutes ago."

She led them to a large round table by a window, where Leslie was already seated, engaged in animated conversation with a couple Abby didn't recognize. Leslie looked up and smiled, her face lighting with pleasure.

"I'm so glad to see you!" she exclaimed as Abby approached. "And you brought reinforcements. Hi, Mike. Hey, Tyler!"

Tyler high-fived Leslie before sliding into the chair next to her. "Ms. Leslie, did you know Ms. Marshall might have a secret room in her attic that might have treasure in it?"

Leslie played along seamlessly. "I've suspected it for years. Maybe if you help with the renovation, you'll be the one to find it."

Tyler's eyes widened at this possibility. He looked to his father for confirmation. "Can I help, Dad? Please?"

Mike ruffled his son's hair affectionately. "We'll see, buddy. There'll be some days when it's safe for you to visit the site."

Introductions were made around the table. Besides Leslie, Emma, Mike, and Tyler, there was a young couple, Ben and Sarah Cooper, who taught at the local elementary school. Sarah, it turned out, was Tyler's second-grade teacher from the previous year.

"Tyler was one of my star students last year," Sarah shared, smiling at the boy who was now busily coloring on the children's menu. "He convinced the entire class to raise money for the animal shelter after their field trip there. Organized a whole penny drive himself."

"He's very persuasive when he wants to be," Mike agreed, pride evident in his voice.

Abby found herself studying Mike and Tyler's interactions, touched by the obvious bond between them. Mike was attentive without hovering, affectionate without being overly demonstrative. He clearly respected his son as an individual, not just an extension of himself.

Conversation flowed easily as they ordered and waited for their food. The topics ranged from the upcoming Laurel Ridge Summer Festival, to Tyler's baseball team, which was undefeated so far this season, to a new book club starting next month at the local bookstore, The Book Nook. Abby was surprised at how quickly she was included in the conversation, with questions directed her way and references to shared history.

"Remember when we all went to that awful school dance sophomore year?" Emma asked, laughing. "And the punch bowl got knocked over?"

"By Jason Matthews, trying to impress Heather Wilson with his dance moves," Leslie added, making air quotes.

"I'd forgotten about that," Abby admitted, the memory surfacing slowly. "Didn't Principal Graves make him mop the entire gym floor?"

"While we all watched from the bleachers," Emma confirmed. "Most entertaining part of the whole dance."

The reminiscing continued, stories building upon stories. Some Abby remembered vividly; others had faded with time. But with each shared memory, she felt more connected to this table of people.

Their food arrived, platters of golden-brown sliced roasted chicken on thick homemade bread, fresh golden french fries, coleslaw, and bowls of gravy for dipping the sandwiches. It was home style cooking at its finest, everything made from scratch with obvious care.

"This is incredible," Abby said after her first bite. "I've missed food like this."

"No good southern cooking in Charleston?" Ben asked.

"Plenty of excellent restaurants," Abby replied. "But it's different when you're eating alone at a trendy place versus sharing a meal like this."

The observation slipped out before she could censor it, revealing more than she'd intended about her life in Charleston. She caught Mike looking at her thoughtfully, but was saved from further explanation by Tyler.

"Ms. Marshall, will you keep the swings on your porch? Dad says old houses are supposed to have porch swings."

"I certainly will," Abby assured him. "That swings have been there since I was a little girl. They need new chains and a fresh coat of paint, but they are definitely staying."

"Good," Tyler nodded, serious as a judge. "Houses need swings so you can watch the stars come out."

"That's exactly right," Abby agreed, charmed by his insight. "It's the perfect spot for stargazing."

"Can I try it sometime? We don't have a porch swing at our house."

Mike intervened gently. "Tyler, remember what we talked about? Ms. Marshall's house is a work site. We need to be respectful of her space."

"It's okay," Abby said. "Tyler is welcome to try out the swings once we get them fixed up. Maybe you both could come for dinner one evening after work? When the kitchen is functional again, of course."

The invitation surprised her as much as it seemed to surprise Mike. His eyebrows lifted slightly, but his smile was warm.

"That's very kind of you," he said. "We'd like that, wouldn't we, Tyler?"

Tyler nodded enthusiastically, mouth full of chicken sandwich.

"I'll help cook," Leslie offered, a mischievous glint in her eye. "Since I know Abby's culinary skills are limited to takeout and microwave popcorn."

"Hey, I've improved," Abby protested. "I can make a very respectable pasta sauce now."

"Ooh, pasta," Tyler perked up. "That's my favorite."

"Mine too," Abby replied, earning a beaming smile from the boy.

As lunch continued, Abby relaxed into the easy camaraderie of the group. There was something refreshing about conversation that didn't revolve around design trends or client demands. She was asked about her life in Charleston with genuine interest, not as a way to assess her professional status or connections.

When Leslie shared a particularly embarrassing story about their high school chemistry experiment gone wrong, Abby found herself laughing until tears formed. It felt good, liberating, even, to laugh like that, uninhibited and genuine.

"I haven't laughed that hard in ages," she admitted, dabbing at her eyes with her napkin.

"That's Charleston's loss," Mike said quietly, his gaze meeting hers across the table. Something in his expression, warmth mingled with admiration, sent a flutter through her chest.

This is dangerous territory, a cautionary voice warned in her head. *Don't get pulled in by a charming single father and friendly small-town dynamics. You have a plan. Stick to it.*

Mike Hatfield was undoubtedly the kind of man she could fall for if she let her guard down. Kind, capable, and genuinely a good man. Add in his obvious devotion to his son and the way his eyes crinkled when he smiled, and he was downright dangerous to her carefully constructed plans.

Because no matter how warm and welcoming Laurel Ridge felt today, Abby knew the truth: this wasn't her life. She had built something in Charleston—a career, a reputation, and connections. The setback at Reed Interiors was just that, a temporary setback, not a sign that she should abandon everything she'd worked for.

And Mike deserved better than someone who was just passing through. He and Tyler had built a stable life here, rooted in community and continuity. The last thing they needed was attachment to someone who would inevitably leave.

As lunch wrapped up and the group began to disperse, Abby stepped outside with Mike and Tyler. Leslie, Sarah, Ben, and Emma had lingered inside to chat with Lily, leaving the three of them momentarily alone on the sidewalk.

"Thank you for including us," Mike said. "It's been a nice Sunday afternoon."

"It was fun," Abby said, meaning it. "Your son is wonderful, Mike. You've done an amazing job raising him."

Mike's expression softened. "Thank you. That means a lot." He glanced down at Tyler, who was crouched on the sidewalk, examining an anthill with fascination. "He makes it easy to be a good dad. He's got a big heart."

"Like his father," Abby said.

Mike looked up, surprised by the compliment. Their eyes met, and for a moment, Abby felt a deepening of connection, a possibility opening.

"Ms. Marshall, look!" Tyler's exclamation broke the moment. He was pointing at the anthill, where a line of ants was diligently carrying crumbs. "They're working together, just like we're going to do in your house!"

Abby crouched beside him, grateful for the distraction. "You're right, Tyler. Teamwork makes the dream work, right?"

"That's what Dad always says," Tyler nodded vigorously. "He says we can do hard things if we work together."

"Your dad is very smart," Abby said, meeting Mike's gaze again over his son's head.

The tenderness in Mike's expression sent a warning flare through Abby's resolve. This was exactly what she needed to avoid, this sense of connection, of potential.

Standing abruptly, she brushed imaginary dust from her dress. "I should be going. I've got work to finish before tomorrow."

"The big demo day," Mike nodded, his expression shifting back to professional. "We'll be there bright and early, 8 AM sharp."

"Perfect. I'll have coffee ready." Abby turned to Tyler. "It was nice to meet you, Tyler."

"See you tomorrow after school, maybe? Dad said I could come see the house if it's ok with you," he said.

"If Ms. Marshall says it's okay," Mike added quickly. "And only for a brief visit. Some areas won't be safe."

Abby felt herself softening again. How could she deny that eager face? "Of course you can visit. I'd like that."

As she walked back to her car at the church, Abby's thoughts were in turmoil. The morning had been unexpectedly pleasant, from the comforting church service to the warm welcome of old and new friends at lunch. For a few hours, she'd felt a sense of belonging that had been notably absent in her life in Charleston.

And then there was Mike. Seeing him with Tyler, witnessing his easy integration into the community, observing the respect others had for him, it all painted a picture of a man who was everything she should be avoiding. Stable. Rooted. Genuinely kind without agenda or artifice.

In six months, you'll be back in Charleston, launching your own design firm. Don't get distracted by small-town charm or attractive single fathers or cozy Sunday lunches.

Yet as she parked in front of Aunt Gertrude's house, another thought whispered through her defenses: *But what if there's more for you here than just a house to renovate? What if Pastor Whitman was right about God preparing unexpected places?*

Abby pushed the thought away. She had design boards to complete, emails to send, a plan to follow. Tomorrow, the real work would begin, transforming this house into a marketable property that would fund her future in Charleston.

That was the goal.

That was the plan.

And no matter how appealing Mike Hatfield's smile was or how charming his son was or how welcoming this community seemed to be, Abby Marshall was sticking to her plan.

She had to.

Chapter 10

"The first hit is yours," Mike said with a grin, handing the sledgehammer to Abby. "Homeowner's privilege."

Abby adjusted her safety goggles and hard hat, feeling slightly ridiculous in the oversized protective gear. She'd dressed for demolition in old jeans and a faded college t-shirt, but somehow Mike managed to make his own work clothes look good. Worn jeans that fit just right and a simple gray t-shirt that stretched across his shoulders as he moved.

"I've never actually demolished anything before," she admitted, hefting the heavy tool. "Unless you count accidentally knocking over a client's vase once."

"Nothing to it. Just pick a spot and swing." Mike gestured to the section of wall they'd marked for removal. "This isn't load-bearing, so you can't do much damage—well, except to the wall, which is the point."

Abby gripped the handle, positioned herself in front of the wall, and swung. The first blow of the sledgehammer resounded through the house with a satisfying crack. Dust billowed from the impact point where the kitchen wall had stood for nearly a century.

"Not bad," Mike nodded.

"Don't sound so surprised," Abby laughed, brushing plaster dust from her sleeve. "I'm stronger than I look."

Abby handed the sledgehammer back, oddly exhilarated by the simple act of destruction. There was something viscerally satisfying about physically breaking down something to rebuild it better.

"Kitchen first," Mike said to two men on his crew as they stood around the demolition-ready space. "We'll gut it completely, check for any hidden issues, replace the plumbing and electrical, then rebuild it into a new kitchen. Abby's design calls for moving the sink to under the window and extending the counters along this wall."

Darrell, a stocky man in his forties with salt-and-pepper hair, nodded as he studied the plans. "Plumbing shouldn't be a problem. That old cast iron waste pipe needs replacing."

Jason, younger and lankier with a quick smile, was already setting up a large wheeled debris bin. "What about those upper cabinets? All coming down?"

"All of them," Abby confirmed. "We're going with open shelving on that wall, custom cabinets on the others."

Work began in earnest then, the kitchen filling with the sounds of demolition: sledgehammers hitting walls, the screech of nails being pulled, the crash of old cabinetry being dismantled. Abby alternated between helping where she could and documenting the process with her camera.

"I've been meaning to ask," Mike said during a brief pause while Darrell and Jason carried a section of countertop outside. "What exactly are you planning for the kitchen design? I've seen the basics of your plans, but I'd like to get a better feel for your vision now that it's finalized."

Abby pulled out her tablet and opened her design portfolio. "I'm thinking of honoring the Victorian era while making it functional," she explained, showing him renderings she'd created. "Custom cabinetry in a sage green with burnished copper hardware. Marble countertops or a good quartz that mimics marble if I need to cut costs. The back splash will be white subway tile with dark grout to give it some definition."

Mike leaned closer to see the screen, bringing with him the scent of cologne, clean and masculine, that made Abby momentarily lose her train of thought.

"That'll look great with the natural light from the windows," he noted, seemingly unaware of her distraction. "What about the floor?"

"Hexagonal tile in white with sage green accents and dark grout as well," she said, swiping to the next image. "It'll tie in with the cabinets and feel period-appropriate."

"You've really thought this through." There was genuine admiration in his voice.

"That's my job," Abby replied with a slight shrug, though his praise warmed her. "Creating cohesive spaces that honor a home's history while making them livable for today."

"It's more than a job for you, though, isn't it?" Mike glanced up from the tablet to her face. "I can hear it in your voice when you talk about design. It's a passion."

Abby felt momentarily transparent under his perceptive gaze. "Yes," she admitted. "I love what I do. Even when it's challenging or clients are demanding, there's nothing like seeing a space transformed, knowing you helped create something beautiful and functional."

A crash from across the room interrupted their conversation as Jason removed the last of the upper cabinets. Dust billowed, revealing the original plaster wall beneath.

"Look at that," Mike called out, moving closer to inspect the exposed wall. "Are those...?"

"Drawings," Abby finished, following him. Beneath decades of cabinets, faint pencil marks were visible on the plaster, childish sketches of what appeared to be a house and stick figures.

"Someone's artwork got preserved when they installed these cabinets, probably back in the sixties, judging by the style," Mike said, gently brushing away dust to reveal more of the drawing. "Looks like a family."

Abby traced the outlines with her finger. "Wow, I wonder if Aunt Gertrude drew this."

Mike looked at her in surprise. "Or a sibling of hers?"

"Maybe. My aunt and uncle never had children of their own, though they wanted them. I bet it was one of Uncle Wilburn's nieces or nephews." She stared at the crude stick figures, a taller one with what might have been a dress, a figure with what looked like a pipe, and a smaller figure between them. "I wonder who drew this. It's adorable."

"We should preserve it," Mike said immediately. "We can frame it out, cover it with clear acrylic."

The suggestion caught Abby off guard. Her practical side thought it was a needless complication to the renovation, but something deeper resonated with the idea.

"Can we really do that? Won't it look strange with the new design?"

"Not at all. We can incorporate it as a memory nook, maybe with some shelving around it. People love that kind of personal history in a home." He watched her reaction carefully. "Unless you'd rather not."

Abby studied the childish drawing, feeling an unexpected wave of emotion.

"Let's keep it," she decided. "You're right... it adds character."

Mike smiled, the corners of his eyes crinkling. "I'll make sure we work it into the design."

By noon, the kitchen was completely gutted, and Abby was covered in a fine layer of dust. Mike's crew had worked efficiently, filling the debris bin and hauling out old cabinetry, countertops, and drywall.

"Perfect timing," Leslie announced, appearing in the doorway with several paper bags. "I come bearing lunch! Figured you all would be ready for a break."

"Leslie, you're a lifesaver," Abby said gratefully, pulling off her hard hat and goggles.

"Martha's sandwiches," Leslie confirmed, holding up the bags. "And her delicious potato salad. I told her you were starting demolition today, and she insisted on sending enough to feed an army."

"That woman is a treasure," Mike said, wiping his hands on a rag before accepting a bag. "Thanks for bringing this over."

"My pleasure. Wanted to see how the demolition was coming along, anyway." Leslie said as she looked around the gutted kitchen with satisfaction.

They moved to the front porch for lunch, the spring air a refreshing change from the dust inside. Darrell and Jason took their sandwiches to eat in their truck, giving Mike, Abby, and Leslie the porch to themselves.

"So," Leslie began, unwrapping her sandwich, "how's the first day going?"

"Productive," Mike answered. "No major surprises yet, which is always good news in an old house."

"We found a child's artwork hidden behind the cabinets," Abby added, explaining about the drawings.

"Wow, how cool!" Leslie exclaimed. "Like a little time capsule. Are you going to keep it?"

"Mike suggested preserving it as a feature," Abby said. "It's actually a nice idea."

"Of course, it's a nice idea. Mike's full of them." Leslie shot him an approving smile. "He did something similar for the Whitakers when they renovated their dining room, preserved a section of wallpaper where all the grandkids' heights had been marked over the years."

Mike shrugged modestly. "Houses have stories. Seems a shame to erase them completely, even when updating."

"That's a lovely way to think about renovation," Abby said.

As they ate, they enjoyed the warm spring day from the shelter of the porch. Birds sang in the massive oak trees that shaded the front yard, and somewhere down the street, a lawnmower hummed.

"This place has good bones," Mike observed, looking out at the garden and back at the house. "Your uncle knew what he was doing when he built it."

"He loved this house," Abby said. "I remember him talking about the importance of properly sized rooms and the flow of space. He said a good house should hold you without confining you."

"Smart man," Mike nodded. "You can feel that philosophy in the layout. The rooms are generous but not cavernous, and there's a natural progression from one to the next."

Leslie glanced between them, a slight smile playing at her lips. "Well, I should get back to the shop," she announced, gathering her lunch wrapper. "Promised Mrs. Hilton that her anniversary arrangement would be ready by three."

After Leslie left, Abby was more conscious of being alone with Mike. He seemed to be deep in thought as she glanced over at him.

"I bet your aunt must have been proud of you," Mike said after a moment. "Seeing you succeed in a field connected to what Wilburn loved so much."

The observation surprised Abby. She'd never explicitly made that connection herself. "I guess it is a continuation of sorts, isn't it? I never thought about it that way."

"Family legacies come in all forms," Mike said. "Tell me more about the firm in Charleston you worked for?"

Abby sighed, the memory still fresh. "Reed Interiors. I was there for seven years, worked my way up to senior designer and then partner. It seemed stable, prestigious even." She shook her head ruefully. "Turns out David Reed was better at spending money than managing it. The bankruptcy announcement blindsided everyone."

"That's rough," Mike said sympathetically. "Seven years is a long investment."

"The worst part is feeling like I should have seen it coming," Abby admitted. "There were signs, now that I think back on it... delayed vendor payments, postponed raises. I just trusted that David knew what he was doing."

"That's not on you," Mike said firmly. "Your job was design, not auditing the company finances."

"I suppose. It still feels like seven years of my life down the drain, though."

"Not down the drain," Mike countered. "You built a portfolio, refined your skills, and made connections. That doesn't disappear with the firm."

"That's true. And it pushed me to consider starting my own business more seriously, which I might never have done otherwise."

"There you go," Mike smiled. "Sometimes what looks like an ending is really a beginning in disguise."

"That sounds almost like something Pastor Whitman would say."

"He probably has," Mike chuckled. "My dad used to say something similar whenever he faced setbacks in his business."

"How long have you had Hatfield House Doctors?" Abby asked, realizing she knew little about his professional background.

"About ten years now," Mike answered. "Started small, just me and a secondhand truck, taking whatever renovation jobs I could get, while still working full time for another company and side jobs for my dad. Then, about eight years ago, it really started taking off, and I focused more on my own business."

"And now you have a crew and a reputation," Abby observed. "That's impressive."

"Laurel Ridge and the surrounding communities have been good to me," Mike said simply. "Word of mouth is everything in a small town. Do good work, treat people fairly, and the business grows."

Abby was struck by his lack of pretension. In Charleston, success was something to be flaunted, achievements prominently displayed. Mike spoke of his business growth with the same casual tone he might use to discuss the weather.

"Is it difficult managing your business as a single parent?"

A shadow crossed Mike's face, but he didn't seem offended by the question. "Sometimes, it's very hard," he admitted. "It was extremely difficult after Tyler was a newborn. I was grieving, sleep-deprived, trying to keep everything afloat while figuring out how to be both mom and dad and my business was taking off."

"I'm sorry," Abby said, regretting bringing up such a painful topic. "I shouldn't have asked."

"It's okay," Mike assured her. "It's part of who I am, part of my story. Those early days were brutal, but the community stepped up in ways I'll never be able to repay. Meals appeared on my doorstep. Clients were understanding when I had to reschedule. Martha, and others I trusted, stepped right up and helped me care for Tyler when I had to work. Eventually, I found my footing, adjusted the business to work around Tyler's needs."

"He's a lucky little boy."

Mike shook his head. "I'm the lucky one. Having him gave me a reason to get up every morning. He saved me. Without him, I could have gone done a very dark hole and never came out."

The depth of emotion in his voice touched something in Abby. This was a man who understood the meaning of true love and sacrifice, who had faced devastating loss and emerged stronger, but not harder.

"Speaking of Tyler," Mike continued, checking his watch, "he's pretty excited about stopping by after school today, if that's still okay with you."

"Of course," Abby said quickly. "I'd love to have him visit. Though I'll warn him, it's pretty dusty right now."

"He'll consider that a feature, not a problem," Mike laughed. "Eight-year-old boys aren't exactly known for their cleanliness standards."

They gathered their lunch things and headed back inside, where Darrell and Jason were already returning to work. The brief respite had reset the energy, and demolition continued with renewed vigor.

Chapter 11

Throughout the afternoon, Abby found herself more and more impressed with Mike's approach to the work. He was hands on, working alongside his crew rather than simply directing. He communicated clearly, explaining his reasoning when making decisions about electrical placement or supporting beams. And he continued to involve Abby at every step, asking for her input and explaining technical details without condescension.

"We'll need to replace all this pipe," he showed her, pointing to an area beneath where the sink would go. "The cast iron's corroded pretty badly."

"Whatever you think is best," Abby nodded. "I trust your judgment."

Mike looked pleased at that, a small smile playing at the corners of his mouth.

By three o'clock, the kitchen had been completely gutted down to the studs, debris removed, and the space swept clean. The afternoon sunlight streamed through the windows, illuminating the now-empty room.

"Looks worse before it looks better," Mike said, surveying their work. "But this is good progress for day one."

"It's exciting," Abby said, visualizing the finished kitchen. "I can already see how much more functional it will be with the new layout."

"Your design's solid," Mike said. "Good balance of aesthetics and practicality."

"I'm excited to see it come together."

"Dad! Ms. Marshall!" Tyler's voice rang out from the front of the house. "Anybody home?"

Mike smiled at the sound. "Back here, buddy! Did you thank Mrs. Perkins for dropping you off?"

"Yes," Tyler said as he appeared in the doorway, backpack still on, eyes wide with excitement. "Whoa! You wrecked it."

"Sure did," Mike agreed.

Tyler entered the gutted kitchen cautiously, taking it all in.

"Where will you cook now, Ms. Marshall?" Tyler asked, looking concerned.

Abby smiled. "I've set up a little temporary kitchen in the dining room, microwave, coffeemaker, and a mini fridge."

"Dad said he was going to bring our camping stove from home for you. He said you might need it."

Abby glanced at Mike in surprise. He shrugged, looking slightly embarrassed. "Figured it might come in handy. It's in the back of my truck. It's propane, so you can use it on the back porch for simple cooking. Better than just a microwave for weeks."

"That's... incredibly thoughtful," Abby said, touched by the gesture. "Thank you."

"Can I see the rest of the house?" Tyler asked eagerly. "Dad said there's a tower room!"

"There is," Abby confirmed. "It was my favorite spot as a little girl. Let me give you the tour."

For the next twenty minutes, Abby led Tyler through the house, showing him the various rooms. Mike followed along, occasionally adding comments about the work they'd be doing. Tyler asked endless questions, his curiosity and enthusiasm infectious.

When they reached the turret room on the third floor, Tyler's face lit up. "This is like a wizard's tower!"

The circular room was small but charming, with windows all around offering views of the town and distant mountains.

"I used to pretend I was a princess in a castle up here," Abby admitted, smiling at the memory.

"What are you going to make it into?" Tyler asked.

"I'm not sure yet," Abby said. "Maybe a reading nook or a small office."

"You should make it a star-watching room," Tyler suggested seriously. "With a telescope and star maps on the ceiling."

"That's actually a pretty cool idea. The views would be perfect for it."

"Tyler has a thing for astronomy right now," Mike explained. "We've been reading books about constellations before bed."

"The stars tell stories," Tyler informed her gravely. "Ancient ones that people have been telling for thousands of years."

"Really?" Abby said, impressed by his knowledge. "My uncle taught me some constellations when I was about your age. We used to sit on the porch swing, and he'd point them out on clear nights."

"You could do that again," Tyler said, as if it were the most obvious thing in the world. "When your swings are fixed."

"Maybe. Let's head back downstairs. I think your dad probably needs to wrap up for the day."

As they descended the stairs, Tyler chattering about stars and planets, Abby felt a curious blend of emotions. There was something undeniably appealing about the image he'd inadvertently painted—evenings on the porch, and tracking stars across the night sky.

Back in the kitchen, Darrell and Jason were packing up their tools. "We're all set here, Mike," Darrell reported. "Everything's prepped for tomorrow's electrical and plumbing work."

"Great job today, guys," Mike nodded.

The men nodded and said their goodbyes, including a polite farewell to Abby. As they left, she realized the day was winding down, and she felt an unexpected reluctance to see it end.

"So, what's on the agenda for tomorrow?" she asked, prolonging the conversation.

"Electrical rough-in for the kitchen," Mike explained. "Our electrician, Frank, will be here to run new circuits and place outlets and switches according to your design. Plumbing work will be started. I'll be working on opening up that doorway between the kitchen and dining room to widen it, and prepping for the new window installation."

"Sounds like another busy day."

"That's the plan," Mike agreed. "Though probably less dusty than today."

"Dad, can we put up the stove for Ms. Marshall before we go?" Tyler asked.

"Sure, if Abby wants us to."

"That would be great," Abby said, "but only if you have time. I know you most likely need to get home."

"It'll just take a few minutes," Mike assured her. "Tyler, why don't you get it out of the truck while I wash up?"

While Mike washed dust from his face, hands, and arms at the utility sink in the basement, Tyler retrieved the camping stove from their truck. Abby followed him to the back porch, where he proudly displayed the compact two-burner unit.

"Dad and I use this when we go camping at New River Gorge," he explained, carefully setting it on the small outdoor table Abby had placed on the porch. "It works really good for pancakes."

"I'll keep that in mind," Abby smiled. "Though I'm not great at pancakes."

"Dad makes the best pancakes," Tyler informed her. "He could teach you. We have them every Saturday morning with blueberries or chocolate chips."

"That sounds like a nice tradition," Abby said, trying to ignore the unbidden image of Saturday morning breakfasts with Mike and Tyler, sunlight streaming through windows, laughter, and easy conversation while sitting around a dining room table enjoying the morning.

Mike interrupted her thoughts as he joined them, demonstrating how to connect the propane tank and light the burners. "It's pretty straightforward," he explained. "Just make sure this valve is turned off completely when you're done. And never use it indoors, of course."

"I promise to be careful," Abby said. "And really, thank you. This will make the next few weeks much more bearable."

"It's no trouble," Mike assured her. "Actually, there's a small cooler in the truck too, if you'd like to borrow it. Might come in handy if your mini fridge gets crowded."

Again, Abby was struck by his thoughtfulness. It was a small gesture, but it spoke volumes about his character, the way he anticipated needs, offered help without being asked.

"That would be great," she accepted. "I bought some groceries yesterday and have been playing refrigerator Tetris ever since."

Tyler ran to fetch the cooler while Mike and Abby stood somewhat awkwardly on the porch.

"Thank you for today," Abby said finally. "For the demolition and... well, everything. You have a real gift for making a stressful process feel manageable."

"It's what I do," Mike replied with a modest smile. "But I'm glad it feels that way. Renovation should be exciting, not just stressful."

"It is exciting," Abby agreed. "Seeing the possibilities, imagining what this place will become."

Tyler returned with the cooler, setting it down with a flourish. "It keeps things really cold for days," he announced. "We tested it on our camping trip."

"Thank you, Tyler," Abby smiled. "Between this and the stove, I'm practically glamping instead of roughing it during the renovation."

Tyler looked confused. "What's glamping?"

"Glamorous camping," Abby explained. "All the fun of being outdoors, but with more comforts."

"Like when Dad brings the air mattress instead of sleeping bags?" Tyler asked.

"Exactly," Abby laughed.

"We should probably head out," Mike said, checking his watch. "Tyler's got homework, and I promised him tacos for dinner."

"Tacos!" Tyler pumped his fist in celebration. "With extra cheese?"

"Would I make them any other way?" Mike ruffled his son's hair affectionately.

"You could come have tacos with us," Tyler suggested. "Dad makes enough for leftovers, anyway."

Abby saw Mike's eyes widen slightly in surprise at his son's impromptu invitation.

"That's very kind of you, Tyler," she said gently, "but I've got some work to finish up here tonight."

"Oh," Tyler's face fell momentarily before brightening again. "Maybe next time?"

"Maybe, but thanks for inviting me."

"We should let Ms. Marshall get back to her work," Mike said, placing a hand on Tyler's shoulder. "We'll see you tomorrow, Abby."

"See you tomorrow," she echoed. "And thanks again for the stove and cooler. It's really above and beyond."

"Happy to help," Mike said simply. "That's what friends do."

Abby remained on the porch as they drove down the driveway, the word friends echoing in her mind.

Chapter 12

Thunder cracked overhead as Abby hurried up the front porch steps, her arms laden with coffee and pastry bags. Rain poured down in sheets, drenching the bottom of her jeans despite her quick dash from the car. She fumbled with the door handle, trying not to spill the coffee.

"Here, let me help with that," Mike said, swinging the door open from within. Water dripped from her hair onto her face as she stepped inside.

"Thanks," she said. "I thought I could beat the storm. Clearly, I was wrong."

Mike took the coffee carrier from her hands. "Perfect timing, actually. Frank just called. He's running late because of the weather."

"Is everything okay?" Abby asked as she pushed her damp hair back from her face.

"Nothing serious, just a tree blocking the road. He'll be here in an hour or two." Mike glanced out the window at the darkening sky. "This might be a blessing in disguise. I wanted to talk through some adjustments to the dining room expansion before we start removing that wall."

"Adjustments?" Abby frowned. "Is there a problem?"

"Not exactly a problem, more of an opportunity." He gestured toward the kitchen. "Let me show you."

Abby followed him to the demolished kitchen. Despite the storm's gloom, the gutted space felt oddly bright without the heavy cabinets and dark walls that had enclosed it for decades. Mike set the coffees on a stack of lumber and pulled a rolled set of plans from a cardboard tube.

"So I was looking more closely at this wall between the kitchen and dining room," he said, spreading the plans on a makeshift table of sawhorses and plywood. "The original idea was to widen the doorway, right?"

"Right," Abby confirmed, stepping closer to see the plans. "To create better flow between the spaces."

Mike nodded, their shoulders nearly touching as they both leaned over the blueprints. "What if we did something more dramatic? This isn't a load-bearing wall. We could remove it entirely, creating one large, open space."

Abby studied the plans, visualizing the change. "That's a significant departure from what we discussed."

"It is," Mike agreed. "But I think it would transform how the space functions. The dining room gets the morning light, and the kitchen, the afternoon sun. Opening it completely would make both spaces feel larger and brighter all day."

Abby bit her lip, considering. The idea had merit. She'd designed open-concept kitchens for clients in Charleston and knew how popular they were. But it would mean rethinking parts of her carefully crafted kitchen design.

"What about the butler's pantry?" she asked, pointing to the small pass-through space adjacent to the dining room. "Would that stay?"

"Absolutely. That's original to the house and has those beautiful built-ins. We'd preserve that completely." Mike pulled out a pencil and lightly sketched on a transparent overlay. "See, we'd remove just this section, leaving the architectural details intact."

Abby watched his hands as he drew—steady, confident strokes that revealed both technical precision and creative vision.

"I like it. It would make entertaining easier, and it honors the way people live now while preserving the home's character."

"Exactly what I was thinking."

"But," Abby added, taking a step back, "it will affect the cabinet layout I designed. And potentially the lighting plan."

"True. Would that be a deal-breaker for you?"

Abby considered this for a moment, taking one of the coffees from the carrier and popping off the lid to let it cool. The scent of rich coffee filled the space.

"No," she decided. "Not a deal-breaker. Actually, it might be better. I could extend the island, add more seating on the dining room side." Her mind was already reconfiguring the space, seeing new possibilities. "The pendant lights would need to be repositioned..."

"I knew you'd see the potential."

"Don't look so smug," she said, but she was smiling too. "You're creating more work for both of us."

"Better to decide now than after we've put in the new door frame," Mike pointed out, taking a sip of his coffee. "Thanks for this, by the way. Perfect on a rainy morning."

"Seemed like the least I could do after you set me up with a camping kitchen." Abby opened one of the pastry bags. "I got an assortment from Martha. She insisted I take the cinnamon rolls because apparently they're your favorite. Martha sure does know everything about everyone. That's one thing I had forgotten about small towns. Everyone knows everything."

"Does that bother you? The 'everyone-knowing-everything' part of small-town life?"

Abby leaned against the makeshift table, considering the question. Outside, rain pattered steadily against the windows, creating a cozy cocoon around their conversation.

"Kind of. In Charleston, there's anonymity. No one knows I'm 'that girl whose parents left' or 'Gertrude's charity case.'"

"Is that how you think people see you or remember you here?" Mike asked.

Abby stared into her coffee. "It's how I felt growing up. After my parents left, there were whispers and always pitying looks. Some kids were cruel back then too, but the adults were worse with their well-intentioned sympathy."

Mike nodded, encouraging her to continue.

"Gertrude and Wilburn were amazing," Abby clarified quickly. "They never made me feel like a burden. But outside this house..." She shrugged, trying to appear more nonchalant than she felt. "Let's just say I was glad to leave for college. I always felt like I was never good enough."

Mike was silent for a moment, seeming to weigh his words carefully. "For what it's worth, that's not how people talk or think about you. People mention your success, and how proud Gertrude was of you."

"Really?" Abby couldn't keep the surprise from her voice.

"Really," Mike confirmed. "Martha was telling me just the other day how Gertrude would come into the diner with magazines that featured your designs, showing them to anyone who'd look."

"I never knew that."

A particularly loud crack of thunder made them both jump, followed by a flickering of the construction lights strung through the space.

"That was close," Mike said, glancing out the window. "Let me check the weather report. We might need to adjust today's plan if this keeps up."

He pulled out his phone, frowning slightly as he checked the forecast. "Looks like this is settling in for the day. Flash flood warnings for the county."

"Will that affect the work schedule?" Abby asked.

"Possibly. We can still do some interior work."

As if on cue, the lights flickered again, more pronounced this time.

"Maybe I'll focus on planning today," Abby said. "I can rework the kitchen design based on the open concept idea."

Mike nodded. "That makes sense. I'll go ahead and work on this wall removal."

They settled into a comfortable rhythm of work despite the storm raging outside. Abby cleared a space in the dining room, spreading out her design materials and sketching new layouts for the kitchen. Mike worked nearby, carefully removing baseboards and crown molding that would be reinstalled later, measuring and marking the wall for demolition.

The rain created a soothing background soundtrack, interrupted occasionally by rumbles of thunder that seemed to be moving further away. The house felt cocoon-like, just the two of them working in companionable near-silence, focused on their respective tasks but aware of each other's presence.

After about an hour, Abby looked up from her sketches to find Mike studying the ceiling in the kitchen with a concerned expression.

"Everything okay?" she asked.

He pointed to a small discolored spot. "Not sure."

Abby stood, coming to look where he indicated. The ceiling plaster showed a faint yellowish spot about the size of a dinner plate. "I don't remember seeing that before."

"Me neither." Mike frowned. "And given this rain, I'm concerned it could be an active leak."

As if to punctuate his worry, a drop of water fell from the stain near the wall, landing with a small splash on the floor.

"That's definitely an active leak," Abby said.

"I need to check the upstairs floors and then the attic," Mike said, already moving toward the stairs. "That's right below where the second-floor bathroom should be."

Abby followed him up the curved staircase to the second floor. The bathroom in question was directly above the spot where they'd seen the leak. Mike pointed to a spot on the ceiling, water slowly dribbling down the wall.

"Let's check the attic," he said.

They continued up to the third floor and then to the small door that led to the attic. Mike pulled the cord for the bare bulb that illuminated the space, revealing the dusty, timber-framed expanse under the roof.

"Watch your step," he cautioned as they entered.

The attic was musty and dim, despite the light bulb. Rain drummed loudly on the roof just overhead. Abby followed carefully behind Mike as he moved toward the area that would be above the leak.

"There," he said, pointing to where water was clearly dripping through a small gap in the roof sheathing near the wall. A puddle had formed on the attic floor.

"Is it serious?"

"Not catastrophic," Mike assessed, "but definitely needs immediate attention."

Another crack of thunder sounded, closer this time, and the light in the attic flickered ominously before going out completely.

"Perfect," Abby muttered in the sudden darkness.

"Hold on," Mike said. A moment later, the beam of a flashlight cut through the gloom. "Always keep one in my pocket on job sites."

The flashlight illuminated his face from below, highlighting the strong line of his jaw and the concern in his eyes.

"We need a bucket or something to catch the water. And I should get up on the roof and apply some quick dry emergency sealant."

"On the roof? In this weather?" Abby shook her head. "That seems dangerous."

"Not while it's actively storming," Mike clarified. "But as soon as there's a lull. Otherwise, this leak could get much worse and cause more damage to the ceilings and walls... all the way down to the first floor."

They fashioned a makeshift water catchment system using a plastic tarp and bucket from Mike's supplies, positioned to catch the dripping water. By the time they finished, both were dusty and slightly damp from the humid attic air.

They made their way carefully back down the attic stairs.

"I've got some battery-powered work lights in my truck," Mike said as they reached the second floor. "Let me grab those so we can see what we're doing."

"I'll check downstairs to see if the leak has gotten any worse," Abby offered.

They parted at the bottom of the stairs, Mike heading out to his truck while Abby returned to the kitchen. Using her phone's flashlight, she examined the ceiling stain. It had grown slightly larger, but the dripping seemed contained in the same spot.

The front door opened, bringing a gust of rain-scented air as Mike returned with several battery-powered LED work lights. He set them up quickly, creating pools of brightness in the shadowy space.

"The leak's a bit bigger, but not dramatically," Abby reported.

Mike nodded, checking his phone. "The radar shows the heaviest bands of rain moving through in the next hour. If the pattern holds, there should be a break after that."

"Enough time for you to safely check the roof?" Abby asked skeptically.

"Should be," Mike said. "I've got roof patch material in the truck. It's not a permanent fix, but it will get us through until we can properly repair it."

The lights he'd set up cast long shadows across the gutted kitchen, creating an oddly intimate atmosphere despite the cavernous space. Abby became aware of a slight chill and rubbed her arms.

"You're cold," Mike observed. "Here."

Before she could protest, he'd shrugged out of his flannel shirt and held it out to her, leaving himself in just a white t-shirt.

"I'm fine, really," Abby started to say, but Mike shook his head.

"You're shivering. It's the dampness from the rain and the attic. The power's out, so the heat isn't running."

Abby accepted the shirt, slipping it on over her own thin top. It was warm from his body and smelled faintly of that same clean cologne she'd noticed before.

"Thanks, you won't be cold?"

"I run hot," Mike said with a slight smile. "Occupational hazard from physical labor, I guess."

The shirt was far too large for her, the sleeves extending well past her fingertips, but she found herself appreciating its warmth and weight.

"So what now?" she asked. "We wait for the storm to pass?"

"Pretty much," Mike confirmed.

"Seems like the renovation is facing its first real challenge," Abby observed.

"Every renovation has its hurdles," Mike said philosophically. "Weather, supply delays, unexpected findings behind walls. The trick is to be flexible and have contingency plans."

"Is that your secret?" Abby asked, settling onto a stack of lumber. "Always having a backup plan?"

"That, and accepting that some things are beyond my control," Mike said, sitting across from her on an overturned bucket.

"That's a good life philosophy in general," she said.

"Took me a while to learn it," Mike admitted. "After Cora died, I tried to control everything... Tyler's schedule, my business, every minute of every day. I thought if I could just manage everything perfectly, I could keep any more pain at bay."

"That must have been exhausting."

"It was. And ultimately impossible. I had to learn to trust again... trust in God's plan, and trust that good things could still happen even if I couldn't control the outcome."

His words resonated with something deep inside Abby. Hadn't she been doing the same thing in her own way? Controlling her environment, her career, and keeping people at a safe distance to avoid the pain of abandonment again?

"I'm still working on that trust part," she admitted.

"Aren't we all?" Mike said with a gentle smile. "So, tell me about your plans after the renovation is complete."

Abby traced a pattern in the dust beside her. "Sell the house and use the proceeds to start my own design firm in Charleston. That's what makes the most sense to me right now. My contacts are in Charleston, and my entire professional network."

"Makes sense," Mike agreed, his expression unreadable.

"What about you?" Abby asked. "Any big plans for Hatfield House Doctors?"

"I've been considering expanding a bit, maybe taking on more historical preservation projects in the surrounding counties. I thoroughly enjoy breathing new life into homes and buildings with stories to tell."

"Like this one," Abby said, glancing around at the exposed beams and lathe of the gutted kitchen.

"Exactly like this one," Mike agreed. "Houses like this were built to last, with craftsmanship you rarely see in new construction. Your uncle understood that. His buildings around town all have that same quality of timelessness."

"He believed in building for generations, not just for the present," Abby said, remembering Wilburn's patient explanations of why certain woods were chosen, why ceiling heights mattered, and how a house needed to breathe and settle with the seasons.

"Smart man," Mike said. "That's becoming a lost art in a world of quick builds and flip properties."

The rain had lessened considerably, now a gentle patter rather than the driving downpour it had been. Mike rose from his seat and moved to the window, his gaze fixed on the clouded sky, his thoughts elsewhere.

"What's on your mind?" she asked, watching him.

He turned to face her, his expression thoughtful. "Something you said earlier. It's been bothering me."

"Oh? What was it?"

"You referred to yourself as a 'charity case' and mentioned people seeing you as 'that girl whose parents left her.' I realize I don't actually know much about what happened to you when you were a little girl."

Chapter 13

Abby's fingers tightened around the hem of Mike's borrowed flannel shirt. The question hung in the air between them, heavy.

"My parents." She exhaled slowly. "Not exactly my favorite topic of conversation."

Mike leaned against the windowsill, his expression open but not pushing. "We don't have to talk about it."

"No, it's..." Abby shook her head, surprising herself with the realization that she actually wanted to tell him. "It's just been a long time since anyone's brought it up."

After a moment, she continued.

"I was ten. A child living in a bad situation on the wrong side of town. It was just a normal Tuesday after school. I remember that because we had art class on Tuesdays, and I'd made this ceramic pinch pot that I was so proud of." She gave a short, humorless laugh. "It's funny, the details that stick with you."

Mike settled back onto the overturned bucket, giving her his full attention.

"I got off the school bus and walked to our trailer. We lived in Shady Creek Park, about twenty minutes outside of town." Abby's throat tightened at the memory. "It wasn't much, but it was home... it was all I knew. I walked inside the trailer like normal after school, and my parents were gone. I remember thinking the trailer felt odd. Quiet and still. At the time, I thought maybe my parents had gone somewhere, which wasn't odd because I was often left home alone."

"At ten years old?" Mike asked, his brow furrowed.

Abby shook her head. "Yes. My parents were alcoholics. There were many times when they just left me on my own, and they'd be off doing whatever they did." She swallowed hard. "But that Tuesday, I just knew something was off."

Mike's expression darkened, but he remained silent, letting her continue.

"I sat in that trailer for hours. I did my homework. Watched TV. I fixed myself a bowl of cereal when I got hungry. I remember I fell asleep on the couch."

She looked up to find Mike watching her, his eyes reflecting the warm glow of the battery-powered lights.

"I woke up the next morning. I remember thinking I should go to school, but I didn't. I remember starting to get scared," she continued. "I went outside and sat on the steps later that day, and it started raining, kind of like today, actually. Eventually, Mrs. Potts from the trailer across the street saw me and brought me inside her home. She made hot chocolate and called the sheriff's department."

"Did your parents leave a note or anything?" Mike asked.

"Nothing. They just left. The sheriff came, asked me questions I couldn't answer. Where might they have gone? Did they mention any plans? Had they been acting different? I didn't know. I was ten." She shrugged, aiming for nonchalance but falling short. "They went inside our trailer and looked around."

A crack of thunder punctuated her words, making them both jump slightly.

"The police found out later that my dad had lost his job the week before. They'd closed their small bank account and withdrew what little money they had, and... then they were gone."

Mike shook his head slowly, his jaw tight. "I can't imagine. You were just a child."

"There's still this part of me that wonders what I did wrong. What made me so easy to leave behind? I mean, how does a parent do that?"

"You didn't do anything wrong, Abby, I'm sure of it."

She nodded. "Anyway, there was a flurry of activity after that. Social services. Foster care discussions. Then Gertrude and Wilburn stepped in." Her expression softened. "I didn't really know them before that. My parents always kept me away from what little family I had here. They were my dad's aunt and uncle. They lived in this beautiful house that seemed like a palace to me..."

"And they took you in," Mike prompted gently.

"They did more than that. They..." Abby paused, emotion welling unexpectedly. "They saved me. Not just from foster care, but from believing I wasn't worth loving."

Outside, the rain continued its steady rhythm, a soothing backdrop to the painful memories.

"Neither one of them ever said a bad word about my parents, even though they had every right to." Abby traced a pattern in the dust beside her. "I remember Gertrude saying that some people aren't equipped for certain challenges of being a parent, and that didn't make my parents bad people."

"That sounds like Gertrude," Mike said with a small smile. "She always saw the best in everyone."

"She did. Almost to a fault." Abby shook her head. "But I wasn't as forgiving. I was so angry for so long. At them for leaving, at myself for not being enough to make them stay. I had this fantasy that they'd come back for me once they got settled somewhere else."

"Did they ever try to contact you?" Mike asked.

"No." The word fell like a stone between them. "Not once. No calls, no letters, no child support, nothing. It's like they erased me from existence." She gave a brittle laugh. "The irony is, when I left for college, I was so determined to reinvent myself. New city, new friends, no one who knew me as 'poor Abby with no parents.'"

Mike leaned forward, elbows on his knees. "Is that why you never moved back here after college?"

"Yes. In Charleston, I'm just Abby Marshall, a successful interior designer. Not Abby Marshall, the girl from the trailer park whose parents didn't want her." She sighed. "But it was also about proving something. That I could be successful, and independent. That I didn't need anyone."

"And, have you? Proven it, I mean."

"I thought I had." Abby's gaze drifted to the window, where raindrops chased each other down the glass in jagged, glistening trails. "But when the firm collapsed, everything I'd built vanished overnight. It was as if my entire life had been swept away by some invisible tide, leaving me stranded exactly where I began—that same abandoned little girl with nothing. Like my identity had been yanked out from under me all over again."

Mike fell silent, weighing her words carefully. When he finally spoke, his voice carried a quiet conviction beneath its gentleness. "You know that's not who you are, don't you? Your worth was never contained in your business card or your zip code."

"Intellectually, sure." Abby offered a small, self-deprecating smile. "Emotionally? I'm still working on that part."

A gust of wind rattled the windows, drawing their attention momentarily to the storm outside. The rain had slackened slightly, but the sky remained dark with clouds.

"For what it's worth, the Abby Marshall I see is extraordinary, regardless of any job title. What your parents put you through was unconscionable, and I'm truly sorry you had to endure that. I understand why you might think people judge you or see you only through the lens of your past, but Abby..." He paused, choosing his words carefully. "Most people have good hearts. I don't believe they see you as some charity case. What I see instead is how remarkable it is that you survived something that could have destroyed you. God protected you from spiraling down a darker path. Your life could have taken such a different turn if you'd remained in that environment you grew up in until you were ten years old, but look at who you've become despite it all."

"I know. I've thought about that before. I am thankful my aunt and uncle took me in and gave me a good life, but it's very hard as an adult to forget what my parents did. I imagine I'll always question my worthiness. But, thank you. What you said really means a lot, especially coming from someone who seems to have it all figured out."

Mike laughed, the sound rich and genuine. "Me? I'm just making it up as I go, like everyone else."

"You seem pretty put-together to me," Abby said. "Single dad, business owner, respected community member."

"Trust me, it's all an illusion," Mike said with a wry smile. "Behind the scenes, it's a lot of frozen pizza, last-minute science projects, and praying I don't forget Tyler's baseball practices and game schedules."

Abby smiled. "Well, you fake it convincingly."

"I've had practice." Mike's expression hardened, a shadow crossing his face. "After Cora died, I felt like every pair of eyes was waiting for me to shatter—though looking back, that was mostly in my head. I became an expert at projecting stability, crafting this perfect façade even when I was hanging by a thread underneath. It wasn't even about fooling others anymore after a while, it was about proving to myself that I could weather anything. Whatever life hurled at me, I refused to break."

The unexpected confession created a bridge between them, two people who understood what it meant to rebuild after loss, to craft a façade of strength when you felt anything but strong.

"How did you get through it?" Abby asked.

Mike considered the question, his gaze turning inward. "One day at a time, honestly. Having Tyler meant I didn't have the luxury of falling apart completely. And the community here..." He gestured vaguely toward the window, indicating the town beyond. "People showed up. Casseroles appeared in my kitchen. Ray Dawson mowed my lawn for the entire first summer. The community and church set up a rotation of people to help with Tyler when he was a baby."

"That sounds nice," Abby said, a hint of wistfulness in her voice.

"It was more than nice. It was essential." Mike looked directly at her. "That's the thing about small towns that you miss in the city. Yes, everyone knows your business here, and yes, there's gossip. But when life falls apart, those same people who whisper or are curious about you are also the ones who show up with a hot meal and a shoulder to cry on."

Abby nodded, thinking of Leslie's immediate support when she'd returned, and Martha's warm welcome at the diner. Perhaps she'd been so focused on the potential judgment that she'd forgotten the flip side of small-town life—the built-in support system, the sense of belonging to something larger than yourself.

"I think I forgot that part," she admitted. "When I left for college, I remember feeling like everyone was talking about me, pitying me, and just waiting for me to fail."

"Certain people probably were," Mike acknowledged. "But Abby, people genuinely cared about you then, and still do. Gertrude made sure of that."

Abby raised an eyebrow. "What do you mean?"

"Gertrude was fierce about protecting you. She'd shut down gossip instantly if she heard it... which honestly didn't happen much. She made it clear to everyone that you were her daughter in every way that mattered, and anyone who suggested otherwise would answer to her."

"Really?"

"Trust me, the whole town knew not to cross Gertrude Marshall when it came to you."

"I miss her," she said. "Every day."

"She was special," Mike agreed. "One of a kind."

There was an undeniable pull toward this quiet, competent man who wore his integrity as naturally as others wore designer labels. Who had listened to her painful story without platitudes or discomfort? Who had, without fanfare, offered her his shirt when she was cold, and set up a camping stove so she could cook during the renovation.

The realization was unsettling. She didn't do attachment. She'd learned that lesson at ten years old, reinforced it through years of carefully managed relationships that never went too deep, and never risked too much. Even her social circle in Charleston consisted largely of professional connections and casual friends—people she enjoyed but could leave behind without too much pain if necessary.

Mike was different. He didn't offer pity, he'd offered understanding. Instead of advice, he'd given validation.

It was disconcerting. And dangerous. Because, for the first time since returning to Laurel Ridge, Abby wondered what it might be like to stay.

Chapter 14

Abby wiped her forehead with the back of her hand and surveyed the chaos surrounding her in her aunt Gertrude's bedroom. Cardboard boxes in various states of fullness, piles of clothing sorted for donation, and stacks of books she couldn't bear to part with yet.

The sounds of construction echoed from downstairs, where Mike and his crew were continuing to work in the kitchen and dining room.

Abby pulled open the top drawer of the mahogany dresser that had stood in this room for as long as she could remember. Gertrude's scarves lay neatly folded inside, a rainbow of silk and cotton squares that still carried the faint scent of her aunt's lavender perfume. She lifted them out, one by one, memories washing over her with each pattern she recognized.

The blue one with tiny roses that Gertrude wore to church on Easter. The autumn-hued paisley she'd wrapped around her neck on cool October mornings. The Christmas plaid she'd donned each December without fail.

Abby placed them in the "Keep" box, then moved to the next drawer. More clothing, more memories, more decisions about what to save and what to let go. By the time she reached the bottom drawer, her eyes were burning from unshed tears.

She slid the last drawer open and paused. Unlike the others, this one contained a photo album bound in faded green fabric and a wood box. Abby lifted both out carefully and settled on the edge of the bed.

The first page of the album held a formal portrait of Gertrude and Wilburn on their wedding day in 1960. Gertrude was radiant in a modest lace gown, and Wilburn beamed in his dark suit. Abby traced their faces with her fingertip, the youthful versions of the people who had saved her.

She turned the pages slowly, watching their lives unfold in snapshots, their first little house together as a couple, numerous holidays and vacations at the beach and other places around the world. And then, there she was: a solemn-faced ten-year-old with tangled hair and wary eyes, standing between Gertrude and Wilburn on the front porch of this very house.

Abby stared at the image, barely recognizing herself in that wounded child. She remembered that day in fragments, the sheriff's cruiser pulling up to the house, Gertrude hurrying down the steps with arms outstretched, and the overwhelming size of the bedroom they'd prepared for her.

She closed the album, unable to look at more, and set it aside on the bed.

The box was made of walnut, its surface adorned with intricate floral carvings. A small brass latch held it closed, but no lock secured it. Abby ran her fingers over the wood, wondering why she'd never seen it before.

With a sense of trepidation, she flipped the latch and lifted the lid.

Inside were stacks of papers—letters, documents, newspaper clippings—along with a few small objects. On top lay a small notebook bound in worn leather, the pages slightly yellowed with age.

Abby lifted it out, immediately recognizing Gertrude's handwriting on the first page. It wasn't a formal journal, more a collection of thoughts and notes, dated sporadically over many years. The first entry was dated just weeks after Abby had come to live with them.

October 12, 2005

Abby called for her mother again last night. She woke crying. What do you tell a child whose parents have simply vanished? Wilburn says time will heal, but I wonder. Looking into Abby's eyes, I see such confusion, such hurt. Lord, give us wisdom to help this child. And if it be Your will, watch over her parents, wherever they may be.

Abby's throat tightened. She turned the page.

November 3, 2005

Sheriff Tompkins called today. No new information on Rick and Donna's whereabouts. Their trail went cold in Tennessee. How does someone just disappear? Abby is settling back into school, but I see the way she watches the road, hoping. Wilburn built her a window seat, hoping to give her some comfort as she watches the driveway, waiting for them to come home. Perhaps I shouldn't encourage this watching and waiting, but I can't bear to take away her hope entirely.

Abby blinked back tears, memories surging of hours spent in that window seat, watching for a car that never came. She'd forgotten that detail—how Wilburn had built it especially for her, how Gertrude had sewn cushions covered in fabric with tiny yellow daisies.

She continued reading; the entries jumping forward in time.

March 15, 2006

Contacted a private investigator today. Wilburn thinks I'm being foolish, throwing good money after bad people, as he puts it. But I disagree. Abby deserves to know what happened to them, even if the truth is painful. And they deserve a chance to make amends if they're able. The Bible teaches forgiveness. Even if I struggle with my own anger at what they did to that precious child.

Abby's hands trembled as she flipped through more pages, scanning entries that documented Gertrude's quiet, persistent efforts to locate her parents over the years. There were notes about phone calls to police departments in different states, letters to social service agencies, even a reference to hiring a second investigator when the first found nothing.

The entries grew less frequent as the years passed, but they never stopped completely. The last one was dated just months before Gertrude's death.

January 4, 2023

Another year begins. Abby is thriving in Charleston, according to her letter that came with her Christmas card. So proud of all she's accomplished, but I worry she's still running from the past. Perhaps that's for the best. My latest inquiry yielded nothing new. After all these years, I'm beginning to accept I may never know what became of Rick and Donna. I pray they found peace, and that someday Abby can find peace with them too. Not for their sake, but for hers.

Abby closed the journal, her vision blurred with tears. She'd had no idea, not the slightest inkling, that Gertrude had spent decades searching for her parents. Her aunt had never mentioned it, never hinted at these ongoing efforts.

Setting the journal aside, she began to examine the other contents in the box. Among them was an official-looking letter on the Department of Social Services letterhead, dated just weeks after she'd come to live with Gertrude and Wilburn. Abby unfolded it with unsteady hands.

Dear Mrs. Marshall,

Following our conversation yesterday, I'm writing to provide the additional information you requested regarding your niece's case. While much of this is sensitive in nature, as Abigail's legal guardian, you have the right to all pertinent background information that might help you provide appropriate care.

As discussed, the circumstances of Rick and Donna Marshall's abandonment of their daughter are complicated by their history of substance abuse. While Abigail was aware of their alcohol dependency, our interviews with neighbors and their former employers indicate a more extensive pattern of drug use as well, primarily methamphetamine and prescription opioids. This addiction likely contributed significantly to their erratic behavior and ultimate decision to leave the area.

The sheriff's department investigation revealed that Rick had been terminated from his employment at Westland Manufacturing because he was found intoxicated and under the influence during his shift for the third time in a month.

Neighbors reported increasing instability in the home environment in the weeks prior to their departure, including late-night disturbances and concerning behavior. One such neighbor, who contacted authorities,

*stated that Donna had appeared "increasingly detached from reality"
in their last few interactions.*

*While none of this excuses their abandonment of their child, it may
help provide a context for their actions. Severe addiction can profoundly
impair judgment and decision-making capacity.*

*Our office has flagged their identities in the national system. Should
they attempt to access social services in another state, we would be notified.
Thus far, there has been no such notification.*

*Regarding your question about Abigail's awareness of these details:
given her age and the traumatic nature of the abandonment, our department psychologist recommends discretion in sharing the full extent
of her parents' substance abuse issues until she is older. A simplified
explanation appropriate to her developmental level would be preferable
at this time, with more detailed information provided when she is older
and better able to process it.*

*I commend you and your husband for providing Abigail with a stable
home during this difficult time. Please do not hesitate to contact me if
you require any additional information or support services.*

Sincerely,
Eleanor Woodson
Senior Case Manager
West Virginia Department of Social Services

Abby stared at the letter, reading it twice more as the implications
sank in. The narrative she'd constructed and carried for two decades,
that of selfish parents who simply didn't want the burden of a child
any longer, was now fractured and reformed into something more
complex, more tragic.

Drugs. Not just alcohol, but serious drug addiction. Methamphetamine. Opioids. Her mother "detached from reality." Her father fired for intoxication.

She set the letter down and reached for another document, a printout of an email from someone named Thomas Reeves, dated 2011.

Mrs. Marshall,

I regret to inform you that my investigation has reached another dead end. The lead in Knoxville did not pan out; the Rick Marshall in question was not your brother-in-law.

After six months of searching, I must be candid about our prospects going forward. Given the time elapsed since their disappearance (6 years) and the lack of any paper trail (no credit cards, property records, tax filings, vehicle registrations, or social security activity), I believe we must consider several possibilities:

1. They are living off the grid, perhaps using assumed identities

2. They have left the country

3. They are deceased

The third possibility, while difficult to contemplate, becomes increasingly likely given the complete absence of official records. Individuals with severe substance abuse issues, particularly those without support systems, face significantly higher mortality rates.

I understand this is not the outcome you hoped for, and I share your disappointment. If you wish to continue the search, I can recommend several avenues, though I caution that they are unlikely to yield different results.

If I can be of any further assistance, please don't hesitate to contact me.

Sincerely,

Thomas Reeves

Reeves Investigations

Abby's hands trembled as she set the email aside. Dead. Her parents might have been dead all this time, while she'd been nursing anger toward them, imagining them living new lives somewhere, and having forgotten her entirely.

She dug deeper into the box, finding more correspondence with investigators, notes from phone calls with police departments, and even a few newspaper clippings about unidentified bodies found in neighboring states. Each one meticulously followed up on by Gertrude, each one ultimately not her parents.

At the bottom of the box lay a small velvet pouch. Abby loosened its drawstring and tipped the contents into her palm: a delicate silver charm bracelet with a single charm, a tiny silver heart. She recognized it instantly. It had been her mother's, one of the few nice things she'd owned and something she had never been allowed to touch. Abby had always admired it as a child, the way it caught the light when her mother moved her hand. She'd thought it lost in the chaos of her transition to Gertrude's home.

The bracelet blurred in Abby's vision as tears welled and spilled. She closed her fingers around it, feeling the cool metal warm against her skin. The simple fact of its existence and that Gertrude had found it, kept it, preserved it for her, spoke volumes about her aunt's compassion.

Through all these documents and the journal, Abby could see that her aunt refused to simplify the complex tragedy of Abby's parents into a story of villains and victims. Gertrude had sought understanding where Abby had chosen judgment. She had pursued reconciliation where Abby had built walls. She had extended grace where Abby had nursed bitterness.

A sob broke from Abby's throat. The first of many as years of carefully controlled emotions finally breached the dam she'd built around them. She curled forward over the open box, clutching the bracelet to her chest, her body shaking with the force of her grief, not just for her lost parents, but for the years she'd spent hardening her heart. For the compassion she might have learned from Gertrude had she been open to it.

She didn't hear the footsteps on the stairs or the gentle knock at the open door. It wasn't until Mike spoke that she realized she was no longer alone.

"Abby? I was wondering if—" He stopped abruptly, taking in the scene before him. "Abby, what's wrong?"

She looked up, unable to speak through her tears. Mike crossed the room in three long strides, concern etched on his features.

"What happened? Are you hurt?" He knelt beside her, his eyes scanning her for injury before settling on her face.

Abby shook her head, struggling to find her voice. "I found—" She gestured helplessly at the box and its contents. "Gertrude kept all this. She was looking for them. All these years."

Understanding dawned in Mike's eyes as he took in the scattered papers. "Your parents?"

Abby nodded, wiping futilely at her tears with her free hand. "She never told me. Not once in twenty years did she mention she was trying to find them."

Mike glanced at the documents, then back at Abby's face. Without a word, he sat beside her on the bed.

"Do you want to tell me what you found?" he asked quietly.

Abby drew a shuddering breath. "They were addicts. Not just alcoholics like I thought. Serious drug addicts—meth, opioids. My mom was 'detached from reality,' according to a neighbor. My dad got fired for being drunk and 'under the influence' at work." She looked down at the bracelet in her palm. "All this time, I thought they just didn't want me. That they were selfish, that they just... left. But they were sick. They were broken people who couldn't even take care of themselves, let alone a child."

Mike was silent for a moment, absorbing her words. "That doesn't make what they did any less painful for you."

"No," Abby agreed, "but it changes... everything. How I've thought about them. How I've thought about myself." She looked up at him, her eyes red-rimmed. "Do you know what it's like to build your entire identity around a story that turns out to be incomplete?"

"I think most of us do that in some way," Mike said gently. "We all have narratives we tell ourselves about our lives, and our pasts. Sometimes, those narratives help us survive. Sometimes they hold us back."

Abby uncurled her fingers, looking at the bracelet in her palm. "This was my mother's. I used to beg her to let me try it on." She closed her hand around it again. "I thought it was lost. But Gertrude had it all this time."

"Wow. It's pretty," Mike said.

"She spent twenty years looking for them. Hired private investigators. Called police departments. Followed up on unidentified bodies." Abby shook her head in disbelief. "Who does that for people who abandoned their child?"

"Someone with a remarkable capacity for compassion," Mike answered. "Someone who understood that people are more than their worst mistakes."

"But why didn't she tell me?" Abby's voice cracked with fresh pain. "Why keep it secret?"

Mike considered the question thoughtfully. "Maybe she was protecting you. Or maybe she was waiting for you to be ready to hear it."

"Ready? I'm thirty years old."

"Age doesn't always equal readiness," Mike said. "And wouldn't you say that you've kept Laurel Ridge, and your past, at arm's length for a long time?"

Abby couldn't argue with that. She had limited her visits home, and kept conversations with Gertrude focused on the present. She always deflected questions about her feelings regarding her parents. She had constructed a life designed to avoid exactly this kind of emotional reckoning.

"There's a letter here," she said, picking up the document, "that says they might have died. Years ago. While I was busy hating them, they might have been dead."

"You couldn't have known," Mike said gently.

"But I could have asked. I could have wondered. I could have shown a fraction of the compassion Gertrude did." Fresh tears welled in Abby's eyes. "Instead, I just... wrote them off. Decided they were monsters who didn't deserve another thought."

Mike was quiet for a moment, his gaze steady on her face. "Can I share something with you? Something from my own experience?"

Abby nodded, wiping her eyes with the back of her hand.

"After Cora died, I was angry. So angry. At God, at the doctors, at myself for not somehow preventing it. I'd lie awake at night going over every moment of her pregnancy, wondering if I'd missed some sign, if I should have insisted on different care." His voice was low, measured, the pain still evident despite the years that had passed. "Pastor Thompson told me something that I didn't want to hear, but that eventually helped me. He said that forgiveness isn't about the other person deserving it. It's about freeing yourself from the burden of carrying that anger."

"Forgiveness," Abby repeated, the word feeling foreign to her tongue. "I'm not sure if I know how to do that."

"It's not a onetime decision," Mike said. "It's a process. Sometimes a long one. And it doesn't mean excusing what happened or pretending it didn't hurt."

Abby looked down at the scattered evidence of Gertrude's decades-long search. "She forgave them."

"And it couldn't have been easy."

"I wish I'd known," Abby whispered. "I wish we'd talked about this while she was alive."

"Maybe finding this now is her way of finally having that conversation with you," Mike suggested. "When you were ready to hear it."

Abby considered his words, finding an unexpected comfort in the idea that Gertrude might have intentionally left these discoveries for her to make when the time was right. It felt like a final gift from her aunt, the truth, with all its complexity and pain, but also with the possibility of healing.

She looked up at Mike, struck again by the kindness in his eyes, the patient way he sat beside her, neither pushing nor retreating from her raw emotion.

"Thank you," she said. "For being here. For not... I don't know, running away when you found me sobbing over a box of old papers."

A small smile touched his lips. "I'm not going anywhere, Abby."

The simple statement carried a weight that settled in her chest, both comforting and terrifying. Because despite her best efforts to maintain emotional distance, Mike Hatfield had somehow slipped past her defenses. And now, in this moment of profound vulnerability, she found herself wanting to lean into that connection rather than pull away from it.

"I came up to tell you we're breaking for lunch," Mike said after a moment. "The crew's heading to Martha's. But I can stay, if you want company."

Abby glanced at the box, the physical evidence of a truth she was only beginning to process. "Would you? Just for a little while?"

Mike nodded, his expression warm. "As long as you need."

She began gathering the papers, organizing them back into the box with careful hands. Mike helped, passing her the journal and various letters without reading them, respecting the privacy of these intimate documents.

As they worked, Abby found herself speaking, the words coming easier than she'd expected. "I've spent so many years being angry at my parents. Proving I could succeed despite them. It became such a core part of who I am—the girl who was abandoned but made something of herself, anyway."

"That part's still true," Mike pointed out. "You did make something of yourself. That strength is real, regardless of the full story about your parents."

"Maybe," Abby conceded. "But what if I've been using that anger as fuel? What if, without it, I don't know who I am anymore?"

Mike considered her question seriously. "I think that's a fear a lot of us have—that if we let go of the things that have defined us, even the painful things, we'll lose ourselves. But in my experience, letting go of anger doesn't diminish you. It makes room for something better."

"Like what?"

"Peace. Joy. Authentic connections with people." He met her gaze steadily. "Forgiveness doesn't mean forgetting who you are. It means discovering who you can be without the weight of all that resentment."

Abby turned the bracelet over in her palm, watching the light catch on the silver heart charm. "I don't even know if they're still alive."

"Does it matter? I don't mean to sound harsh, but... forgiveness isn't about them anymore. It's about you."

The question struck Abby like a physical blow. Did it matter? She'd spent twenty years imagining confrontations that might never happen, closure that might never come. Perhaps the real closure wasn't in finding her parents, but in releasing the hold they had on her.

"I don't know how to start," she admitted.

"Prayer helps," Mike suggested. "Talking to God about it, even if you're not sure what to say."

Abby nodded, though her relationship with prayer was complicated at best. She'd attended church with Gertrude and Wilburn growing up, had even found comfort in faith during those early years after her parents left. But as she'd gotten older, built her career, constructed her independent life, that connection had faded to something more distant, more formal.

"I haven't exactly been the most faithful person," she said with a self-deprecating smile.

"God doesn't keep score," Mike said simply. "He's there when you're ready."

They finished organizing the papers, and Abby closed the wooden box, running her fingers over the carved lid. "I think I need some time to process all this."

"Of course," Mike said, standing.

Abby looked up at him, this man who had entered her life as a contractor but was rapidly becoming something much more significant.

"You should go have lunch with your crew. I'm okay, really. I just need a little quiet time."

Mike studied her face, as if assessing the truth of her words. "Are you sure?"

"I'm sure." She managed a small smile. "Thank you for being here. For listening."

He nodded, moving toward the door, then paused. "Abby? For what it's worth, I think Gertrude would be proud of you right now. Finding the courage to face this, to reconsider what you've always believed—that takes real strength."

After Mike left, Abby sat in the quiet room, the bracelet still clutched in her hand.

She looked around at Gertrude's bedroom, the floral wallpaper her aunt had loved, the lace curtains that filtered the sunlight, the collection of family photos on the dresser that included Abby's high school graduation, her college commencement, and the opening of her first major design project in Charleston.

Gertrude had celebrated every milestone, supported every dream, all while quietly, persistently, searching for her parents. Not out of some misplaced loyalty to them, but out of love for Abby and perhaps out of a Christian compassion that understood the brokenness behind their actions.

For the first time, Abby wondered if her success in Charleston had been as much about running away as it had been about achievement. Had she been so focused on escaping her past that she'd missed the chance to truly heal from it?

The revelation about her parents' addiction didn't erase the pain of their abandonment. If anything, it complicated it, adding layers of tragedy and waste to what had already been a profound loss. But it also opened a door that Abby had kept firmly shut for twenty years, the possibility of understanding, of compassion, and of forgiveness.

She fastened the silver bracelet around her wrist, the heart charm cool against her skin. It felt foreign, yet a tangible connection to a mother she'd tried so hard to forget.

"I don't know if you're still out there," she whispered to the empty room. "I don't know if you ever tried to find me, or if you survived your demons. But I've been carrying this anger for so long, and I'm tired." Her voice broke on the last word. "I'm so tired of being angry."

Tears slipped down her cheeks, but they felt different from the sobs that had overtaken her earlier—cleaner, somehow, less bitter.

"Aunt Gertrude never gave up on you," she continued, the words coming easier now. "She kept looking, kept hoping. I wish I'd known that."

Abby closed her eyes, the bracelet a gentle weight on her wrist.

"God," she said hesitantly, the prayer feeling rusty from disuse, "I don't know how to do this. I don't know how to let go of something I've held on to for so long. But I want to try. Help me try."

She sat in silence for several minutes, listening to the distant sounds of birds outside the window, the occasional car passing on the street below.

Eventually, Abby rose from the bed, placing the wooden box carefully on Gertrude's dresser. She would return to its contents later, read through more of the documents and journal entries when she felt stronger.

Abby caught sight of herself in Gertrude's mirror, eyes red from crying, hair disheveled, her mom's silver bracelet gleaming at her wrist. She hardly recognized the woman staring back at her, so different from the polished, controlled professional she presented to the world.

Yet somehow, this tear stained, vulnerable version of herself felt more authentic than the facade she'd maintained for years. This was Abby Marshall without the armor, without the carefully constructed narrative—just a woman confronting her past.

The sound of vehicles pulling up outside broke into her thoughts. The construction crew returning from lunch, ready to resume their work on transforming the house. Life continuing, moving forward, even as she stood at this profound crossroads of her past and future.

Abby took a deep breath, straightened her shoulders, and turned away from the mirror. She washed her face and composed herself.

As she stepped into the hallway, she heard Mike's voice downstairs, giving instructions to his crew. The sound anchored her somehow, a reminder that she wasn't facing this journey alone. There were people in her life, in this town she'd tried so hard to leave behind, who might walk alongside her if she let them.

She touched the silver heart charm on her wrist and descended the stairs.

Chapter 15

Abby grabbed her purse and walked out the front door.

She walked down the tree-lined driveway onto the streets of Laurel Ridge with purpose.

The walk to Laurel Ridge Community Church took fifteen minutes—fifteen minutes of racing thoughts and a pounding heart. Several times she nearly turned back, questioning her impulse to seek Pastor Andrew, a man she barely knew.

The church stood on a gentle rise at the edge of downtown, its white steeple piercing the blue April sky. Abby hesitated at the bottom of the wood steps, second-guessing herself.

"Just go in," she muttered, giving herself a mental push.

The church's heavy wooden doors were unlocked. Abby stepped into the cool, dim interior, her footsteps echoing on the hardwood floor. The sanctuary beyond was empty, peaceful in its stillness, sunlight streaming through stained-glass to create pools of color on the pews.

"Hello?" she called, her voice sounding unnaturally loud in the quiet space.

A door opened to her left. "May I help you?" A middle-aged woman with a kind face and practical bob emerged from what appeared to be an office.

"I was looking for Pastor Andrew," Abby said. "I don't have an appointment, but I was hoping to speak with him if he's available."

The woman smiled. "You're Abby Marshall, aren't you? I'm Diane, the church secretary." She extended her hand, which Abby shook. "Pastor Andrew is just finishing up a phone call. Why don't you have a seat, and I'll let him know you're here?"

Abby sank onto a cushioned bench near the office door, suddenly aware that her eyes were probably still red from crying. She ran a hand through her hair, attempting to smooth it, and wished she'd taken a moment to compose herself better before rushing over.

The door to the inner office opened, and Pastor Andrew stepped out, his expression warm and welcoming.

"Abby, what a pleasant surprise," he said. "Please, come in."

She followed him into his office, a modest room lined with bookshelves and brightened by a large window overlooking a small garden. He gestured to a comfortable chair across from his desk.

"Can I get you some water? Coffee?" he offered.

"Water would be great, thank you."

As he filled a glass from a small dispenser in the corner, Abby took a deep breath, trying to organize her thoughts. What exactly had she come here for? What did she expect this man to tell her that would somehow make sense of the emotional earthquake she'd experienced?

Pastor Andrew handed her the water and settled into his chair. "I was glad to see you at service on Sunday," he said.

"Yes, it was... nice." Abby took a sip of water, buying time. "Actually, that sermon you gave, about finding your place, it's been on my mind."

Andrew nodded encouragingly, but didn't interrupt.

"Something happened today," she continued, her voice unsteady. "I found... well, I found out that a lot of what I believed about my past isn't entirely true." She twisted the silver bracelet on her wrist, a nervous gesture. "I don't know if you know my background—"

"Only bits and pieces," Pastor Andrew admitted. "I know you grew up here with your aunt and uncle. I remember you vaguely from school, and that you've been living in Charleston for some years."

Abby nodded, oddly relieved. "My parents abandoned me when I was ten," she said, the words coming out more bluntly than she'd intended. "Just... left. No note, no explanation. I came home from school, and they were gone."

Pastor Andrew's expression registered compassion without pity. "I'm so sorry, Abby. That's a profound trauma for anyone, especially a child."

"For twenty years, I've believed they simply didn't want me anymore. That they were selfish, that they just... left." Abby's fingers tightened around the water glass. "Today, I found a box in my aunt's room. She'd been searching for them all these years, hiring investigators, and following leads. And she'd collected information about why they might have left."

She took another steadying breath. "They were addicts. Not just alcoholics, which I knew about, but serious drug addicts—meth, and opioids. According to the reports, my mother was 'increasingly detached from reality' in her last days in town. My father had been fired for being intoxicated and under the influence at work."

Pastor Andrew listened attentively, his gaze steady and kind.

"There's even a possibility they could be dead," Abby continued, her voice catching. "While I've been busy hating them, building my entire identity around being the abandoned child who succeeded anyway, they might be dead."

She set the water glass down with trembling hands. "I don't know what to do with this information. It changes everything and nothing at the same time. They still left me. But the story I've been telling myself about who they were and why they left—it's not that simple anymore."

"Few things in life are as simple as we'd like them to be," Pastor Andrew said quietly. "Especially when it comes to human brokenness."

"My aunt spent twenty years looking for them," Abby said, still incredulous. "Twenty years searching for people who abandoned her niece. Who does that?"

"Someone with extraordinary compassion," Pastor Andrew replied. "Someone who understood that people are more than their worst moments or their worst decisions."

The echo of Mike's earlier words wasn't lost on Abby. "That's almost exactly what Mike said."

A small smile touched Pastor Andrew's lips. "Mike's a wise man. And he's had his own journey with grief and forgiveness."

Abby nodded. "He mentioned something about that," she said. "About forgiveness being for yourself, not the other person."

"There's truth in that," Pastor Andrew agreed. "But I'd add that forgiveness is also about recognizing our common brokenness. None of us lives without failing others or ourselves in some way."

He leaned forward slightly. "Abby, what is it you're seeking today? Understanding? Guidance? A place to process these feelings?"

What was she seeking? She'd come here on impulse, driven by a storm of emotions she couldn't contain.

"I don't know how to forgive them," she admitted finally. "I've spent twenty years being angry. It became part of who I am—the girl who was abandoned but made something of herself, anyway. What if I don't know who I am without that anger?"

Pastor Andrew considered her question thoughtfully. "That's a profound insight, recognizing how our wounds can become part of our identity. But I wonder if what you're really asking is: who could you become with the freedom that forgiveness brings?"

The question hung in the air between them, challenging and hopeful at once.

"The Bible often speaks about forgiveness," Pastor Andrew continued. "Not because it's easy, but because it's essential for our healing. Jesus tells a parable about a servant who's forgiven an enormous debt by his master, but then refuses to forgive a much smaller debt owed to him by a fellow servant. The point isn't that we should forgive because we've been forgiven—though that's part of it. It's also that unforgiveness becomes a prison of our making."

"That's what it feels like sometimes," Abby admitted. "A prison. Especially now, being back here in Laurel Ridge, surrounded by memories and reminders."

"Perhaps that's not coincidental," Pastor Andrew suggested. "Sometimes God brings us full circle to face the things we've been running from, not to punish us, but to heal us."

"I didn't come back here looking for healing," she said. "I came back because my career in Charleston imploded."

"God often works through our practical circumstances," Pastor Andrew said with a smile. "The question isn't so much why you came back, but what you might find now that you're here."

Abby twisted the silver bracelet again, watching the light play on its surface. "I don't even know where to start with forgiveness. It feels impossible."

"It often does," Pastor Andrew acknowledged. "Especially with wounds as deep as yours. But forgiveness isn't a single moment—it's a process, and a journey. And it begins with a choice."

"A choice?"

"To be open to the possibility of seeing things differently. To be willing to let go of the narrative that's defined you, even if you don't know yet what will take its place." He paused. "May I suggest something practical?"

Abby nodded, grateful for any concrete guidance.

"Take some time over the coming days to simply be still with this new information. Perhaps read some passages in Scripture about forgiveness. I'd be happy to suggest a few. Allow yourself to feel whatever emotions arise without judgment. Grief, anger, confusion—they're all natural responses to what you've learned."

He reached for a small notepad on his desk and jotted down several references. "These might be helpful starting points," he said, handing her the paper. "Matthew 6:14-15, Colossians 3:13, Ephesians 4:31-32."

Abby took the note, folding it carefully and tucking it into her purse. "Thank you."

"And perhaps most importantly," Pastor Andrew continued, "give yourself grace. This is a significant revelation that challenges much of what you've believed about your past. It will take time to process."

"Grace," Abby repeated softly. "That's not something I've given myself much of over the years."

"Then perhaps that's the place to start," Pastor Andrew suggested. "Before you can extend forgiveness to your parents, you might need to forgive yourself for the very human response of anger you've carried."

The idea was startling, that she might need forgiveness too, for the hardened heart she'd cultivated in response to her parents' actions.

"You know," Pastor Andrew said, his tone lightening slightly, "sometimes when we're wrestling with something this profound, it helps to step away from it temporarily. To do something entirely different that gives our minds and hearts space to process in the background."

"Like what?"

"Anything that brings you joy or peace. A hike in nature. A day trip somewhere new. Time with a friend doing something fun and uncomplicated." He smiled. "God often speaks most clearly to us when we're not straining to hear."

Abby considered his suggestion. The idea of a brief respite from the emotional intensity of the past twenty-four hours was appealing. "That actually sounds... perfect."

"The journey of forgiveness isn't a sprint, Abby. It's more like a marathon, with rest stops along the way." Pastor Andrew's expression was kind but direct. "And you don't have to run it alone."

The simple statement touched something deep within her, a longing for connection she'd denied for too long. In Charleston, she'd cultivated professional relationships and casual friendships, but kept people at arm's length. Here in Laurel Ridge, despite her best efforts to maintain emotional distance, she was finding herself drawn into a web of caring that both frightened and comforted her.

"Thank you for taking the time to speak with me today," she said, rising from her chair. "This has helped more than I expected."

"My door is always open," Pastor Andrew assured her, standing as well. "And Abby? I'll be praying for you as you navigate this journey."

The walk back to the house was slower, more measured than her urgent journey to the church had been. Abby's mind churned with Pastor Andrew's words, particularly his suggestion about taking a break from the intensity of her emotions.

Maybe he was right. Maybe she needed a few days to step away, to breathe, to do something that had nothing to do with renovation or revelation or the past.

As she approached the Victorian, she noticed Mike's truck still parked out front. Despite her emotional turmoil, or perhaps because of it, she found herself looking forward to seeing him again.

She entered through the front door. Mike was in the kitchen with Darrell, reviewing something on a set of plans spread across the makeshift table of sawhorses and plywood.

He looked up as she entered, concern evident in his eyes. "Hey, are you okay? You left in kind of a hurry."

"I went to see Pastor Andrew," she said, surprising herself with her candor. "I needed to talk to someone about... everything."

Understanding dawned in Mike's expression. "Did it help?"

"I think so." Abby glanced at Darrell, who was diplomatically focusing on the plans with unusual intensity. "Can I talk to you for a minute?"

"Of course," Mike said immediately. "Darrell, can you double-check those measurements for the cabinet installation? I'll be right back."

Darrell nodded, still not looking up. "Take your time, boss."

Mike followed Abby into the living room, which was untouched by the renovation chaos. They sat on opposite ends of the sofa, angled toward each other.

"Pastor Andrew was really helpful. He gave me some Bible passages to look at, and we talked about forgiveness as a process, not a single decision."

Mike nodded encouragingly.

"He also suggested I might need to take a break from all this intensity. Do something entirely different for a day or so, to give my mind space to process everything." She looked up at Mike, suddenly uncertain. "What do you think?"

"I think that's excellent advice," Mike said. "Sometimes you need to step away from a problem to see it clearly."

"The thing is," Abby continued, her voice dropping slightly, "I don't really know what to do around here. All my memories of Laurel Ridge are from high school or earlier, and I haven't exactly been exploring since I got back."

Mike was quiet for a moment, considering. "I have an idea," he said finally. "But it might sound a little crazy."

"I could use a little crazy right now," Abby admitted with a small smile.

"The crew can continue to work on their own. They are all good people and I trust them one hundred percent." Mike leaned forward slightly. "What if we took Tyler and went to Green Valley Adventure Park tomorrow? It's about an hour from here. They've got hiking trails, zip lines, a small lake. Just take a day away from everything, outside in the fresh air."

Abby blinked, surprised by the suggestion. "You want me to go with you and Tyler to an adventure park?"

"Only if you want to," Mike added quickly. "No pressure. Tyler's been asking to go for months." He shrugged. "Plus, I could use a day off, too."

The offer was unexpected but oddly appealing. A day away from adulting. A day of simple enjoyment with Mike and his son, who had shown nothing but kindness to her.

"Will Tyler mind if I tag along?" she asked, hesitantly.

Mike laughed. "Are you kidding? He thinks you're the coolest person ever since you let him explore the 'secret' spaces in this house. He'd be thrilled."

Abby smiled. "Okay, then. Yes. Let's do it."

"Really?" Mike's face lit up with surprise and pleasure.

"Really. I think a day of adventure and fun is exactly what I need. What time should I be ready?"

"I'll pick you up around 8:30?" Mike suggested.

"8:30 it is," Abby agreed. She hesitated, then added, "Thank you, Mike. Not just for tomorrow, but for today. For listening to me and understanding."

Mike's expression softened. "That's what friends do, Abby. They show up."

Friends.

The word felt both inadequate and significant. Because whatever was developing between them, it had already transcended the boundaries of a typical contractor-client relationship, or even a casual friendship.

"I should let you get back to work," she said, standing. "I am going to take the rest of the evening off. I'm not even going to open my laptop or look at the design boards."

Mike rose as well. "Actually, I was about to wrap up for the day." He glanced at his watch. "It's nearly six."

"Oh," Abby said, surprised by how the time had flown. "I didn't realize it was so late."

An awkward moment stretched between them, neither quite ready to part ways.

"Would you like to grab dinner?" Mike asked. "Nothing fancy, just Martha's or maybe Lily's. Tyler's at a friend's house for a sleepover tonight, so I'm on my own."

The invitation was casual, friendly—but Abby couldn't help feeling a flutter of something more in her chest. "I'd like that," she said.

"Great," Mike said, his smile warming his entire face. "Let me just pack up my tools, and we can head out."

As he returned to the kitchen, Abby stood in the middle of her aunt's living room, a strange mix of emotions swirling within her. Grief for what she'd lost, both the parents who had left her and the aunt who had loved her unconditionally. Confusion about how to process the revelations of the day. Anxiety about the path forward.

But alongside these difficult feelings was something unexpected, a quiet spark of hope. Hope that forgiveness might be possible, that she might find healing in this place she'd tried so hard to leave behind. Hope that the connections she was forming, with Mike, with the community, and with her faith, might lead somewhere she hadn't allowed herself to imagine.

She touched the silver bracelet on her wrist, the tangible link to a mother she'd spent years trying to forget. For the first time, she let herself wonder about her parents, not with anger, but with a complicated compassion. Where had their addiction led them? Had they ever found help, or had their demons consumed them? Had they ever regretted leaving her behind?

She might never know the answers. But perhaps, as both Mike and Pastor Andrew had suggested, the answers weren't what mattered most. What mattered was finding a way to make peace with the questions, to forgive even without understanding, and to move forward even if closure never came.

Chapter 16

The sound of Mike returning pulled her from her thoughts. "Ready?" he asked, keys in hand.

Abby nodded, reaching for her purse. "Ready."

Martha's Diner was busy but not packed, the dinner rush just beginning to taper off. Martha herself led them to a booth by the window, dropping menus on the table with a knowing smile that Abby chose to ignore.

"Specials are on the board," Martha said. "And don't even think about rushing off without dessert. I made fresh pies this afternoon."

"Wouldn't dream of it," Mike assured her with a grin.

As Martha bustled away, Abby opened her menu, though she barely needed to look at it. The offerings at Martha's hadn't changed significantly in two decades.

"So," Mike said, setting his menu aside, "adventure park tomorrow. Fair warning: Tyler will probably try to talk you into riding the mega zip line. It's completely safe, but if heights aren't your thing, you might want to prepare your excuse now."

Abby laughed, grateful for the shift to lighter conversation. "Actually, I love heights. I once did a skydiving trip in college."

Mike's eyebrows shot up. "Seriously? You jumped out of a perfectly good airplane?"

"I did," Abby confirmed with a smile. "It was terrifying and exhilarating at the same time."

"I'm impressed," Mike said. "And a little intimidated. Tyler's going to think you're even cooler now."

Their waitress arrived to take their orders—a cheeseburger and fries for Mike, a grilled chicken salad sandwich for Abby, and coffee for both.

"So, this adventure park," Abby said once the waitress had left. "What else should I know about it?"

Mike leaned back in the booth. "It's pretty great, from what I hear. They've got hiking trails through the woods, a couple of small lakes for fishing or paddle boats, the zip line course I mentioned, and some other ropes-course type activities. There's a picnic area, too."

"Sounds like the perfect distraction. I want nothing more than to be a kid tomorrow. Have fun and just enjoy a day of doing whatever."

"That's the idea." Mike studied her face. "How are you doing, really? After everything today?"

Abby appreciated his directness. "I'm okay. Better than I was earlier, at least. Talking to Pastor Andrew helped. And honestly, having plans for tomorrow helps too—something to look forward to that has nothing to do with renovations or revelations."

"I'm glad."

Their food arrived, and conversation shifted to lighter topics, memories of Laurel Ridge, and stories about Tyler's latest school adventures. It was easy and comfortable in a way that surprised Abby. She couldn't remember the last time she'd enjoyed a simple dinner with someone like this, without agenda or pretense.

As they finished their meal, Martha appeared with two slices of warm apple pie à la mode, setting them down with a flourish. "On the house," she declared. "It does my heart good to see you two catching up after all these years. Seeing you both smile is priceless. I hope I see more of it."

Before either could respond, she was gone, leaving Abby and Mike exchanging amused glances.

"I love her," Mike said with a chuckle. "She always makes it a joy to come here and eat."

"And her pie is amazing," Abby added after taking a bite.

"Some things in Laurel Ridge never change," Mike said. "Martha's pie. The way the church bells sound on Sunday morning. The way, everyone knows everyone else's business within about five minutes."

"That last one I hadn't missed," Abby admitted wryly.

"I can imagine." Mike's expression turned thoughtful. "It must have been hard growing up with everyone knowing your story."

Abby considered this, fork poised over her pie. "It was, in some ways. I always felt like I was 'poor Abby' to numerous people. But looking back, I think I probably imagined more judgment than was actually there."

"Kids aren't known for their nuanced understanding of complex situations," Mike said. "I remember when my mom died, I was twelve. For months, I hated the way teachers would look at me with that mixture of pity and awkwardness, like they were afraid I might burst into tears at any moment."

"I didn't know about your mom," Abby said softly.

"Cancer," Mike said. "It was a long battle, almost two years. By the end, it was a relief in some ways, which then made me feel guilty for feeling relieved." He shook his head. "Grief is complicated."

"Yes, it is," Abby agreed, thinking of her own tangled emotions. "Did it get easier? Dealing with people's reactions?"

"Eventually," Mike said. "Or maybe I just got better at navigating it. And some people, like your aunt Gertrude, for example, actually... knew exactly how to be supportive without being smothering."

Abby smiled.

"She brought us meals for weeks after Mom died," Mike recalled. "She never hovered over my dad and me or asked prying questions. She'd just drop off the food, chat with Dad for a few minutes about normal things, and always had a listening ear when we needed it most. It meant a lot."

"She was good at that, knowing what people needed," Abby said, a wave of fresh grief washing over her. "I miss her wisdom now more than ever."

Mike reached across the table, briefly covering her hand with his. "I think she'd be proud of how you're handling all this. Seeking guidance, being open to a new perspective—that takes courage."

The simple touch sent a warmth up Abby's arm that had nothing to do with the coffee she'd been drinking. She met his gaze, struck again by the genuine care she saw there.

"Thank you," she said softly. "For today, for tomorrow, for... understanding."

"You don't have to thank me, Abby, honestly," Mike replied, his voice equally soft. "I'm just glad I was there when you needed someone. And I'll continue to be here for you."

The moment stretched between them, charged with something neither was quite ready to name. Finally, Mike glanced at his watch and reluctantly withdrew his hand.

"We should probably get going," he said. "Early start tomorrow."

Abby nodded, both relieved and disappointed at the break in tension. "8:30, right?"

"On the dot," Mike confirmed with a smile. "And wear comfortable shoes. We'll be doing a lot of walking."

They settled the bill, Mike insisting on paying despite Abby's protests, and stepped out into the cool evening air. The streetlights had come on while they were eating, casting a gentle glow over Laurel Ridge's main street.

"I think I'll walk home if you don't mind. Clear my head a bit," Abby said.

Mike nodded, understanding in his eyes. "Alright. I'll see you in the morning, then."

"I'm looking forward to it."

"Me too," Mike replied with a smile that crinkled the corners of his eyes.

They parted ways, Mike heading toward his truck while Abby turned in the direction of the house. As she walked the quiet streets of Laurel Ridge, she found her thoughts drifting not to the painful revelations of the day, but to the adventure that awaited tomorrow. A day away, in the company of a man who seemed to understand her better than anyone had in a very long time.

Chapter 17

Abby's alarm jolted her awake. She blinked at the ceiling, momentarily disoriented before remembering—adventure park day. A smile spread across her face as she swung her legs over the side of the bed. She'd slept better than expected, the emotional exhaustion of the previous day giving way to a deep, dreamless sleep. As she prepared for the day, her favorite pair of jeans, a light sweater, and comfortable walking shoes, she felt a lightness that had been absent for weeks, maybe months.

At precisely 8:30, the doorbell rang. Abby grabbed her small backpack and hurried downstairs, an unexpected flutter of anticipation in her stomach.

Mike stood on the porch, casual in jeans and a navy Henley that brought out the blue in his hazel eyes. Behind him, practically bouncing with excitement, was Tyler.

"Miss Abby!" the boy exclaimed. "Did you really go skydiving?"

Abby laughed, charmed by his enthusiasm. "I did go skydiving, though it was a long time ago."

"Are you excited about going to the adventure park? We're gonna do the mega zip line," Tyler informed her solemnly. "It's super high and super-fast, and Dad said I'm tall enough to do it."

"I am excited," Abby said, matching his serious tone. "I can't wait."

Mike caught her eye. "Ready for an adventure?" he asked.

Abby smiled, a genuine, unguarded smile that felt like a gift after the emotional turmoil of yesterday. "More than ready," she replied.

The drive to Green Valley Adventure Park passed quickly, filled with Tyler's excited chatter about school, his friends, and his detailed knowledge of every attraction awaiting them. Abby was drawn into his enthusiasm, asking questions and laughing at his animated descriptions.

"Tyler's my adventure park expert," Mike explained as they turned onto a winding road that led deeper into the forested hills. "He's been studying the website for months."

"I made a plan," Tyler announced from the back seat. "For maximum fun."

"Maximum fun?" Abby repeated, amused. "That sounds interesting. So what's first on this plan?"

Tyler leaned forward eagerly. "The flying squirrel course! It's like mini zip lines between platforms in the trees. We should do that before it gets crowded, then stop for a snack, then the hiking trail to the waterfall, then lunch, then paddle boats, and then the mega zip line."

"Sounds like you've thought of everything," Abby said, genuinely impressed by the boy's planning.

"I like to be prepared," Tyler said with a shrug that mimicked his father's.

The resemblance between them was striking, not just in physical features, but in mannerisms and expressions. Abby felt a pang of both admiration and wistfulness. Mike was clearly an exceptional father, attentive and engaged. She wondered briefly what her life might have been like if her parents had been capable of that kind of love and stability.

But today wasn't for dwelling on the past. Today was for "maximum fun," as Tyler would say.

They arrived at the park just as it opened, securing a parking spot close to the entrance. The morning air was crisp and fresh, a perfect Saturday. As they approached the main gate, Abby felt a surge of genuine excitement. It had been too long since she'd done something purely for enjoyment.

Mike insisted on paying for her admission, despite her protests. "This was my idea," he reminded her. "Consider it part of the contractor-client relationship. I occasionally treat valued clients to adventure park outings."

"Is that in the official contract?" Abby teased.

"It's in the fine print," Mike assured her with a wink that sent an unexpected warmth through her chest.

Tyler, impatient with adult banter, tugged at his father's arm. "Come on, Dad! The flying squirrel course is first!"

The morning unfolded according to Tyler's meticulous plan. The flying squirrel course proved to be a series of short zip lines and rope bridges connecting wooden platforms built among the trees. It was less intimidating than Abby had anticipated, but no less fun. Tyler led the way, fearless and agile, while Mike brought up the rear, offering encouragement and the occasional steadying hand when needed.

By the time they completed the course, Abby's cheeks hurt from laughing and smiling. There was something profoundly freeing about being thirty feet above the ground, suspended between trees, focused on nothing more complex than making it to the next platform.

"That was awesome!" Tyler declared as they descended the final staircase back to ground level. "What did you think, Miss Abby?"

"It was fantastic," she agreed, brushing wood chips from her hands. "You're an excellent guide, Tyler."

The boy beamed at the praise. "Next up snack break, then the waterfall hike!"

They found a picnic table near the snack bar, where Mike produced granola bars and fruit from his backpack. As they ate, Tyler peppered Abby with questions about the house renovation, particularly about the turret room that seemed to intrigue him.

"Can I come see it again?" he asked, eyes wide with hope.

Abby glanced at Mike, who gave a small shrug as if to say, "Up to you."

"Of course," she said.

***

The waterfall hike was more strenuous than Abby had expected, the trail winding uphill through dense forest. Tyler bounded ahead like a mountain goat, periodically stopping to examine interesting rocks or point out woodland creatures.

"He's got endless energy," Abby commented as they climbed a particularly steep section.

"Tell me about it," Mike replied with a good-natured groan. "Some mornings I'm barely on my first cup of coffee, and he's already asking to build a treehouse or redesign his bedroom."

They paused at a scenic overlook, catching their breath, while Tyler explored a nearby cluster of boulders under Mike's watchful eye.

"He's an amazing kid," Abby said. "You've done an incredible job with him."

Mike's expression softened. "Thanks. It hasn't always been easy, but he makes it worth it. Every single day."

As they continued up the trail, it narrowed, forcing them to walk single file. At a particularly tricky section with loose rocks, Mike reached back and offered Abby his hand. She took it without hesitation, the warmth of his palm against hers sending a pleasant tingle up her arm.

"Careful here," he said, steadying her as she navigated the uneven terrain.

Their hands remaining connected even after they reached stable ground.

"Dad! Miss Abby! I can hear the waterfall!"

Mike reluctantly released her hand, but the warmth of his touch lingered. The look they exchanged was brief, but charged.

The waterfall was worth the climb, a sixty-foot cascade tumbling over moss-covered rocks into a clear pool below. They found a flat rock to rest on, Tyler skipping smaller stones across the pool's surface while Abby and Mike sat side by side.

"This was a good idea," Abby said, taking in the peaceful setting. "I needed a day like this more than I realized."

"I used to come to places like this after Cora died. Just sit and listen to the water. It helped somehow."

"Nature has a way of putting human problems in perspective," Abby said, watching the sunlight dance on the rippling water.

Tyler approached, plopping down beside them. "I'm starving," he announced dramatically. "Is it lunchtime yet?"

"Almost. Ready to head back down?" Mike asked.

The descent was easier physically, but required more caution. At one particularly steep section, Mike insisted on helping both Tyler and

Abby down, his strong hands steady and reassuring as he guided them over the rough terrain.

"My hero," Abby teased when they reached level ground, though her smile held genuine appreciation.

"Just part of the service," Mike replied with a mock bow.

Lunch was a picnic at one of the designated areas, sandwiches Mike had packed, chips, and cold drinks from the park's concession stand. They found a table under a sprawling oak tree, the dappled sunlight creating patterns on the wooden surface.

Tyler, having wolfed down his sandwich in record time, spotted some children playing nearby. "Dad, can I go play? They're building a fort with sticks!"

Mike assessed the situation—the children were within easy viewing distance, supervised by parents. "Sure, buddy. Stay where I can see you."

After Tyler dashed off, Mike and Abby were alone for the first time that day.

"He's having a blast," Abby observed, watching Tyler introduce himself to the other children with easy confidence.

"He is. But honestly, I think I'm having just as much fun," Mike admitted. "It's nice, doing something like this... with you."

"I'm having fun too," Abby said. "More than I've had in a long time."

Mike's gaze met hers, a moment of connection that made her heart beat a little faster. Then, to her surprise, he chuckled.

"What?" she asked, curious.

"Nothing, just..." He shook his head, looking slightly embarrassed. "If sixteen-year-old me could see this moment, he'd never believe it."

Abby tilted her head. "What do you mean?"

Mike hesitated, then seemed to decide to simply be honest. "I had the biggest crush on you in high school," he admitted. "Not that you ever noticed me. I was just the quiet guy who sat behind you in the Home Ec class my senior year."

Abby's eyes widened. "Wait... you were in one of my classes?" Abby thought back to her conversation with Leslie from last week, when she learned that Mike had harbored feelings for her all those years ago.

"Mrs. Patterson, second period," Mike confirmed with a rueful smile. "I spent most of that semester staring at the back of your head, trying to work up the courage to ask you to prom."

"You wanted to ask me to prom?" Abby was genuinely surprised. "I had no idea."

"Yep, I chickened out. You were...intimidating. Smart, beautiful, confident. And I was just a shy kid who liked to build things and play basketball."

Abby felt a blush warming her cheeks. "I can't believe I never knew."

"You had a lot going on," Mike said. "And anyway, it all worked out. I ended up meeting Cora in college. You built your career in Charleston. Different paths."

"That somehow crossed again," Abby added.

"Dad! Miss Abby!" Tyler's voice broke the moment as he ran back to their table. "They've opened the mega zip line! Can we go now? Please?"

Mike laughed, ruffling his son's hair. "What happened to your carefully planned schedule? Aren't paddle boats next?"

"Plans change, dad," Tyler declared with a grin.

"I'm ready for this mega zip line if you two are," Abby said, standing and gathering their lunch trash.

The mega zip line lived up to its name. A thousand-foot cable stretching across a scenic valley, starting from a platform built atop a seventy-foot tower. As they climbed the stairs to the launch point, Abby felt a familiar mix of excitement and trepidation.

Tyler went first, fearless and exuberant, letting out a whoop of joy as he sailed across the valley. Mike and Abby watched from the platform, both laughing at his unbridled enthusiasm.

"Your turn," Mike said, gesturing toward the waiting attendant who would help her into the harness.

"Are you nervous?" Abby asked, noting his calm demeanor.

"I'm terrified of heights like this, believe it or not," Mike admitted with a sheepish grin. "And somehow, having you here is making this easier."

The simple honesty of his statement touched her deeply. As the attendant helped secure her harness, Abby impulsively reached for Mike's hand and squeezed it. "You've got this," she said. "I'll see you on the other side."

The zip line was exhilarating. The initial drop sending her stomach into free fall before the cable's tension caught her, propelling her forward at thrilling speed. The valley spread beneath her, a patchwork of summer colors and sunlight, and for those perfect moments, Abby felt utterly free.

Mike followed shortly after, his initial white-knuckled grip on the harness giving way to genuine enjoyment as he soared across the valley. When he landed on the platform where Abby and Tyler waited, his face was flushed with a mixture of relief and triumph.

"That was awesome, Dad!" Tyler exclaimed, bouncing with residual excitement.

"It really was," Mike agreed, his eyes finding Abby's.

The rest of the afternoon passed in a blur of activities, a paddleboat ride on the small lake, a visit to the petting zoo section, and finally, ice cream cones. The sun began its descent toward the horizon.

They found a quiet spot on a grassy hill to enjoy their treats, and afterward Tyler fell asleep on the ground beside his dad, obviously exhausted after their fun filled day.

"I'd call today a success," Mike said, watching his son with affection. "Maximum fun achieved."

"Definitely," Abby agreed. "I'm glad you suggested this."

"Me too," Mike admitted. "I haven't taken a complete day off in... I can't even remember how long."

"We workaholics have to stick together," Abby said with a smile.

Mike's expression turned more serious. "You know, Abby, I've been thinking about what you said yesterday, about your parents and forgiveness."

She nodded, encouraging him to continue.

"After Cora died, I was angry for a long time," he said quietly. "Not angry with her—she didn't choose to die. But at God, at the doctors, at the universe. It felt like everything had been taken from me."

"That's understandable," Abby said.

"What helped me eventually wasn't trying to force myself to 'get over it,'" Mike continued. "It was allowing myself to feel all of it, the anger, the grief, the confusion, and then, gradually, finding ways to honor her memory by living fully. Tyler needed me to be present, not perfect."

His hand found hers on the grass between them, fingers intertwining naturally.

"What I'm trying to say is, forgiveness—of others, of yourself, of circumstances—it comes in its time. You can't rush it or force it. But you can be open to it."

Abby looked down at their joined hands, then back up at Mike's face. "When did you get so wise?" she asked, her tone gently teasing but her eyes serious.

"Hard-won lessons," he replied with a small smile. "And lots of therapy."

Tyler's voice interrupted their moment. "Dad, I'm hungry again. Can we get dinner before we go home?"

Mike chuckled. "The bottomless pit is awake." He squeezed Abby's hand once before releasing it. "What do you say? Dinner in town before we head back?"

"I'd like that," Abby said, surprised by how much she meant it.

As they walked back toward the parking lot, Tyler skipping ahead, and Mike held her hand.

Chapter 18

Abby smoothed the edge of the quilt beneath her, breathing in the sweet scent of freshly cut grass. The church picnic had officially ended, but clusters of people still lingered on the expansive lawn behind Laurel Ridge Community Church. Children darted between adults, their laughter carrying in the afternoon breeze. On the makeshift baseball diamond, Mike stood on the pitcher's mound, his easy stance betraying years of practice as he lobbed a gentle pitch toward Tyler.

"That's it, buddy! Keep your eye on the ball!" Mike called as Tyler swung with determined concentration, connecting with a satisfying crack that sent the ball sailing past second base.

Abby couldn't help but smile as Tyler sprinted toward first base, arms pumping and face alight with triumph.

"Someone's enjoying the view," Leslie teased, nudging Abby's shoulder as she settled back onto the quilt beside her. "And I don't mean the baseball game."

"I'm just watching Tyler," Abby protested, though she knew her flushed cheeks betrayed her.

"Mmm-hmm," Martha hummed skeptically as she placed a tray of lemonade glasses on the quilt and lowered herself to sit. "And I'm just here for the refreshments."

Emma laughed, tucking her legs beneath her as she joined them. "Leave her alone, you two. Though I must say, Mike playing baseball is quite attractive... brings back good memories from high school."

"Ladies, please," Abby groaned, accepting a glass of lemonade from Martha while trying to maintain her dignity.

Lily completed their circle, settling beside Emma. "How are the renovations going?" she asked, mercifully changing the subject.

"Good," Abby replied, grateful for the redirection. "The kitchen is completely gutted. New electrical and plumbing throughout the house this coming week. Mike's crew is great."

"I'm sure Mike is giving your project his very personal attention," Leslie said with exaggerated innocence.

The women laughed as Abby rolled her eyes. "You're impossible."

"We just care about you," Martha said. "Both of you, actually. Mike's a good man who deserves happiness, and so do you, dear."

Abby traced the condensation on her glass, suddenly finding it difficult to meet their eyes.

"I made a discovery the other day," she said. "About my parents."

The women's expressions shifted immediately from playful to attentive.

"I found a box in Aunt Gertrude's room," Abby continued. "She'd been searching for my parents for years after they left. Hired private investigators, contacted shelters and hospitals."

Martha nodded. "Gertrude was relentless when she cared about something."

"My parents were both severe addicts," Abby said, the words still strange on her tongue. "Drugs and alcohol. There's no conclusive proof, but they might not even be alive."

"Oh, Abby," Emma murmured.

"The thing is," Abby continued, "I've spent twenty years being angry at them. Building this narrative that they didn't want me. That they abandoned me for some exciting new life. But in reality, they were just... broken people? They had an addiction to something that was far stronger than they were. I started thinking, what if they left because they couldn't stop destroying themselves and didn't want to destroy me too? What if there was some tiny speck of thought in their minds that knew they were destroying themselves, and so they chose to leave to save me?"

Leslie squeezed her arm. "If that was their reasoning, then it was a decent thought."

"I don't know what to do with this information," Abby admitted. "It's like the story I've been telling myself about my life has an entirely different ending than I thought."

"Forgiveness," Lily said. "That's what Gertrude worked so hard for. She was set on not just finding them, but being ready to forgive them when she did."

Abby looked up, surprised. "You knew about this?"

Lily exchanged glances with Martha, who nodded. "Not all the details. But Gertrude, Martha, and I were in the same Bible study group for years. She often spoke about praying for the strength to forgive your parents, not for their sake, but for yours and hers."

"That's what Pastor Andrew said," Abby murmured. "That forgiveness isn't about excusing what happened, but about freeing yourself."

"Wise man, our pastor," Martha nodded approvingly.

"I'm trying really hard," Abby said. "I'm trying to see my parents differently. To forgive. It's just... I've built my entire identity around proving something to people who might not even be alive to see it."

Leslie studied Abby's face. "Is that why you're so determined to go back to Charleston? To keep proving something?"

Abby took a long sip of lemonade, using the moment to gather her thoughts.

"Maybe," she finally admitted. "Charleston was where I reinvented myself. Nobody knew me as the girl her parents didn't want. Nobody pitied me or whispered about my family."

"And now?" Martha prompted gently.

Abby glanced toward the baseball game, where Mike was demonstrating a proper batting stance to Tyler, his hands patiently adjusting the boy's grip on the bat.

"Now I'm not so sure what I'm running toward. Or from. This whole thing with my parents and finding out more about them... it's changed everything."

The women followed her gaze, a knowing look passing between them.

"He's quite taken with you," Lily observed. "Has been since high school, if I recall correctly."

Abby felt heat rise to her cheeks again. "He told me yesterday. About having a crush on me in high school. I never knew it."

"Of course you didn't," Leslie laughed. "You were too busy planning your escape from Laurel Ridge to notice."

"Honey, that boy only had eyes for you when you were in high school," Martha said, chuckling at the memory.

"You're exaggerating," Abby insisted, though she couldn't help smiling at the image.

"Only slightly," Martha conceded with a wink.

"We spent the day together yesterday," Abby admitted. "At Green Valley Adventure Park."

"And?" Leslie prompted, clearly hungry for details.

"And it was... wonderful," Abby said, surprising herself with the simple truth of it. "Easy. Fun. Tyler is amazing, so bright, and curious. And Mike is..." she trailed off, searching for words that wouldn't sound hopelessly smitten.

"Handsome? Kind? Devoted? Talented?" Martha supplied helpfully. "Built like he could carry you and a load of lumber up three flights of stairs without breaking a sweat?"

"Martha!" Lily exclaimed, though her scandalized tone was undermined by her laughter.

Abby buried her face in her hands, unable to suppress her laughter. "You're terrible. All of you."

"We're observant," Leslie corrected. "And we care about you both."

When Abby looked up, their expressions had turned more serious.

"Can I be blunt, dear?" Martha asked, setting down her lemonade.

"When have you ever been anything else?" Abby replied with affection.

"Life is short," Martha said simply. "Painfully, beautifully short. I had many good years with my Scottie before his heart gave out. Years that felt like five minutes when they were over. He's been gone fifteen years now, and I miss him every day."

The group grew quiet, respecting the weight of Martha's words.

"Nothing is holding you to Charleston," she continued. "Your job is gone. The life you built there has already changed. Meanwhile, here you have a house with good bones, a community that loves you, and a man who looks at you like you're the answer to a prayer he was afraid to speak aloud."

Abby's breath caught at the unexpected poetry in Martha's practical assessment.

"You could open your own design business here," Leslie added, warming to the theme. "The nearest interior designer is in Winchester, and half the historic homes in this town could use your expertise."

"That's a big change from what I planned."

"Plans change," Emma said. "Sometimes for the better, and like Martha said, life is short."

A cheer erupted from the baseball field, drawing their attention. Tyler had apparently scored a run and was being congratulated by the other players. Mike caught Abby's eye across the distance, his smile visible even from where she sat.

"Look at that," Lily murmured. "He can't take his eyes off you, even with a baseball game going on."

"It's mutual," Leslie observed, studying Abby's face. "Isn't it?"

Abby took a deep breath. "I think I'm falling for him," she admitted, the words both terrifying and liberating to speak aloud. "Which is completely impractical and probably foolish."

"Or," Leslie countered, "it could be the most sensible thing you've done in years."

"What about my career? My plans?"

"Your career can flourish anywhere with your talent," Emma said. "And plans are meant to guide us, not imprison us."

Martha nodded in agreement. "Sometimes the best adventures come from tearing up the map altogether."

Abby looked back toward the field, where the game appeared to be wrapping up. Mike was collecting equipment while Tyler chatted animatedly with some other children.

"I'm scared," she confessed, turning back to her friends. "What if I stay, and it doesn't work out? What if I'm not cut out for small-town life? What if Mike and I try and fail, and I've given up everything for nothing?"

"What if you don't try and end up spending the rest of your life wondering what might have been?" Lily countered gently.

Leslie took Abby's hand between her own. "Nobody's saying you have to decide today. Take your time. Finish the renovations. Get to know Mike better. See if Laurel Ridge still feels like the place you couldn't wait to escape, or if it might be the home you've been looking for all along?"

"Just promise us that you'll keep an open mind," Emma added. "And an open heart."

Abby squeezed Leslie's hand, grateful for the unconditional support. "I promise, I'll try."

"Good," Martha declared, reaching for the lemonade pitcher. "Now, who needs a refill before those baseball players descend on us like locusts? Because I guarantee they're heading this way, and Tyler alone could drink this entire pitcher by himself."

Chapter 19

The lazy Sunday afternoon stretched on pleasantly, and throughout the day, Abby remained acutely aware of Mike's presence.

As the church gathering began to disperse in the late afternoon, he approached Abby.

"Tyler and I were thinking of getting ice cream at Scoops before heading home," he said, a hint of nervousness in his casual tone. "Care to join us?"

Before Abby could respond, Leslie appeared at her side. "Actually, Abby promised to help me with something at the flower shop," she interjected smoothly. "Rain check?"

Abby shot Leslie a confused look, which her friend pointedly ignored.

"Oh, sure," Mike said, clearly disappointed but rallying quickly. "Another time, then."

"Definitely," Abby assured him. "I had a wonderful time yesterday. And today."

Mike's smile returned, warming his eyes. "Me too. Both days."

After Mike left to collect Tyler, Abby turned to Leslie with raised eyebrows. "What was that about? I didn't promise to help you with anything."

"No, but you need to," Leslie replied cryptically, linking her arm through Abby's as they walked toward the parking lot. "Trust me on this."

"Trust you on what?"

"The art of anticipation," Leslie said with a knowing smile. "Mike is smitten with you. Making him wait one more day to spend time with you won't hurt him."

"That's ridiculous," Abby protested.

"It's strategy. Besides, I really do need your help with something."

Twenty minutes later, Abby was in Leslie's apartment above the flower shop, surrounded by photo albums and scrapbooks spread across the coffee table.

"What exactly am I helping you with?" Abby asked, settling onto the couch.

"Perspective," Leslie replied, handing her an album. "Open it."

Abby did as instructed, finding herself looking at photographs from high school. There she was, seventeen and serious, clearly posing reluctantly for the camera in many shots.

"Keep going," Leslie encouraged.

As Abby turned the pages, she began noticing something or rather, someone. Mike, younger and lankier but unmistakable, often positioned where he could see her, his expression a mixture of admiration and wistfulness.

"You're kidding me," Abby murmured, leaning closer to examine a photo from what appeared to be a school dance. She was talking to Leslie near the punch bowl, while in the background, Mike stood with a group of friends, his attention clearly directed toward her rather than his companions.

"Not kidding," Leslie said, sitting beside her. "He wasn't just crushing on you, Abby. He was head over heels."

"I honestly never knew."

"You were focused on escaping," Leslie said without judgment. "On building a future far away from here. You didn't see what, or who, was right in front of you."

Abby continued turning pages, seeing herself through the lens of time and new knowledge. "Why are you showing me this?"

Leslie's expression turned serious. "Because history doesn't have to repeat itself. Because sometimes we get second chances."

Abby closed the album, emotions swirling too rapidly to name. "What if it's just nostalgia? What if he's romanticizing the past?"

"What if he's not?" Leslie countered. "What if this is real, Abby? What if this is exactly where you're supposed to be?"

Abby leaned back against the cushions, processing. "When did you become so philosophical?"

"Around the same time, you became so afraid of happiness."

The words stung with their accuracy. "I'm not afraid of happiness."

"Aren't you? You've built this successful career, this independent life, but when was the last time you were truly happy? Not just accomplished or satisfied, but heart-full, can't-stop-smiling happy?"

Abby opened her mouth to respond, then closed it again, the answer surprising her. "Yesterday," she admitted. "At the adventure park with Mike and Tyler."

Leslie nodded, as if this confirmed something she already knew. "And before that?"

Abby thought carefully. "Maybe... when I secured the big account at Reed Interiors. That was a major win."

"Professional satisfaction," Leslie observed. "Important, but not the same thing."

"What's your point, Leslie?"

"My point is that happiness isn't waiting for you in Charleston. Maybe it's been here all along, in a place you were too determined to leave to even notice."

Abby sighed, running a hand through her hair. "It's not that simple."

"It never is," Leslie agreed. "But that doesn't mean it isn't worth exploring."

"What would you do?" Abby finally asked. "If you were me?"

Leslie considered the question carefully. "I'd give myself permission to want more than I planned. To consider that God has something better in mind than what I mapped out. I'd give myself permission to stop running."

"Even if it means starting over?"

"Especially then," Leslie said firmly. "The most beautiful gardens grow where the ground has been completely turned over."

Abby smiled at the florist's metaphor. "Now you sound like Pastor Andrew."

"I'll take that as a compliment," Leslie laughed. "Though I think my delivery is less sermon-like."

"Marginally," Abby teased.

Leslie stood and moved to the kitchenette. "Tea? I think this conversation calls for something stronger than lemonade."

"Tea would be perfect," Abby agreed.

As Leslie filled the kettle, Abby was drawn back to the photo albums, this time examining them with new eyes, not just seeing her younger self, but noticing the community that had surrounded her even then. Martha, behind the counter at the diner, smiling. Lily helping decorate for a school dance. Aunt Gertrude presenting scholarships at her high school graduation. And Mike, in several of the photos.

"I didn't realize how many people cared about me," she said when Leslie returned with two steaming mugs. "Back then, I felt so alone. I was so focused on making a name for myself, an identity. Like I had to prove I was worth keeping around."

"You never had to prove that," Leslie said, settling beside her again. "Not to anyone who mattered."

"Aunt Gertrude and Uncle Wilburn loved me unconditionally. So did you. So did this whole town, really."

"We still do," Leslie said simply. "That's what community is, Abby. People who see your worth even when you can't."

Abby sipped her tea, letting the warmth and the truth of Leslie's words sink in. "So what now? I just... what? Stay? Give up everything I've built in Charleston?"

"Not give up," Leslie corrected. "Transform. Bring your talents here. Build something new that incorporates the best of both worlds."

"And Mike?" Abby asked, her voice smaller than she intended.

Leslie's expression softened. "That's entirely up to you. But if you're asking my opinion, which you literally did, I think you'd be crazy not to see where this could go. Men like Mike don't come along every day. The good ones are all taken, and for good reason."

"He's... special."

"He is," Leslie agreed. "And so are you."

Abby felt a flutter of something like hope expanding in her chest. "I don't want to rush into anything."

"No one's suggesting you should," Leslie assured her. "Take your time. Finish the renovations. Get to know each other better. Just... stay open to the possibility that your happy ending might look different from what you planned."

"How did you get so smart?"

Leslie smiled, a hint of sadness touching her eyes. "Experience. Not all of it pleasant. I've watched too many people chase what they think they want, only to miss what they truly need."

Abby reached out and squeezed her friend's hand, sensing a story Leslie wasn't ready to share. "Thanks for the perspective and caring enough to kidnap me from an ice cream date."

Leslie laughed, the momentary melancholy lifting. "You can thank me by actually going on a proper date with the man. Soon."

"I'll think about it," Abby promised.

"Don't think too long," Leslie advised. "Some opportunities don't wait forever. Tyler can come spend an evening or a day with me, and you and Mike can go on a real date... alone."

Later that evening, as Abby walked back to the house, her mind swirled with the day's conversations. The women's insights, the photos showing what she'd been too preoccupied to see, Leslie's gentle but firm push toward considering a different future than she'd planned.

As she walked up the driveway, the graceful old Victorian stood solid against the darkening sky, its windows like eyes watching her return. For the first time since arriving in Laurel Ridge, Abby truly saw it not as a temporary project or an investment property, but as a home. Her home, if she chose to make it so.

Her phone chimed with a text message. Mike's name appeared on the screen: *Tyler wanted me to tell you he was sad you couldn't join us for ice cream. So, was I. Renovation meeting tomorrow at 8?*

Abby smiled, typing her response: *Tell Tyler I'm sorry I missed it. Looking forward to tomorrow.*

She hesitated, then added: *And maybe we can reschedule that ice cream soon.*

His reply came almost immediately: *It's a date. Or not. No pressure. Unless you want it to be. I'm making this awkward, aren't I?*

Abby laughed out loud, a warmth spreading through her chest. *Yes, it's awkward. And yes, it's a date. Goodnight, Mike.*

Goodnight, Abby. Sweet dreams.

As she climbed the porch steps, Abby paused to look up at the star-filled sky above Laurel Ridge. The same stars would be visible from Charleston, she knew, but somehow they seemed brighter here, clearer and more numerous against the small-town darkness.

"Maybe this could work," she whispered to the night air.

Chapter 20

Mike balanced the cardboard drink carrier in one hand while knocking on Abby's front door with the other. He shifted his weight from one foot to the other, suddenly aware of the nervous energy coursing through him.

The door swung open, and there was Abby in jeans and a simple blue t-shirt, hair pulled back in a casual ponytail.

She took his breath away.

"Morning, you didn't have to knock... I mean, you work here after all, and I was expecting you," she said, her smile bright but carrying a hint of something he couldn't quite read. "Perfect timing, though. I just finished reviewing the electrical plans for the tenth time."

"I'm early, I know, but I come bearing gifts," Mike replied, lifting the drink carrier. "Two coffees—yours with hazelnut creamer—and Martha's cinnamon rolls —still warm."

"You are so thoughtful," Abby said as she stepped back, ushering him inside.

The foyer was cluttered with sample boards and material swatches, the organized chaos of a designer at work. Mike followed her to the kitchen. New drywall had been installed, though it awaited primer and paint. The custom cabinets were scheduled for delivery tomorrow.

"I can't believe how quickly this is coming together," Abby said, clearing a space at the makeshift worktable. "The electrical inspection is scheduled for next Wednesday, right?"

"Yes, and plumbing on Thursday if all goes well." Mike placed their breakfast on the table and took the seat across from her. "My crew will be here around nine today to continue working on the electrical and plumbing on the first floor. I'm going to work on finishing the drywall here in the kitchen."

Abby nodded, taking a sip of her coffee. Her eyes closed briefly in appreciation. "Perfect. Thank you for this."

"My pleasure." Mike watched as she broke off a piece of cinnamon roll, struck by how comfortable sharing breakfast felt, discussing the day's work. It was easy to imagine more mornings like this, stretching into years.

He reined in his thoughts.

"So, what's on your agenda today?" he asked, trying to keep his tone casual. "Paint samples? Fixture selection?"

Abby hesitated, her fingers tracing the rim of her coffee cup. "Actually, I'm taking the day off."

"Oh?" Mike tried to hide his disappointment. He'd been looking forward to working alongside her today.

"I need some time to think," she said, meeting his eyes directly. "Some space to process everything that's going on in my life. The house, my parents, Laurel Ridge... and you."

Her honesty caught him off guard. "Me?"

A soft blush colored her cheeks. "Yes, you. This... whatever this is between us... it's unexpected. Good, unexpected, but still..."

"I understand," Mike said, and he did. "Taking time to sort through your thoughts is smart."

"You're not upset?"

"Why would I be upset about you taking care of yourself?" He smiled, hoping to reassure her. "Besides, absence makes the heart grow fonder, right?"

Her laugh eased the moment. "Is that what you're hoping for?"

"Can't blame a man for trying," he admitted, earning another laugh.

They finished their breakfast, discussing the renovation timeline and material deliveries expected for the coming week. Throughout their conversation, Mike noticed a quiet determination in Abby's manner, as if she'd made some internal decision he wasn't yet privy to.

When they'd finished, she walked with him to the front door. At the threshold, she surprised him by reaching for his hand.

"Thank you for understanding," she said, her fingers warm against his. "Not just about today, but about... everything."

"That's what friends do," Mike replied.

"Is that what we are? Friends?" Her question held no challenge, just genuine curiosity.

Mike considered his answer carefully. "I think we're becoming something more than friends, Abby. But whatever we are, whatever we might be, it has to unfold at the right pace for both of us."

Relief and something warmer flickered in her eyes. "I'll see you later?"

"Count on it."

He watched as she gathered her purse and keys, then followed her outside. She climbed into her car, rolling down the window before starting the engine.

"Wish me luck," she said, a nervous edge to her smile.

"For what?"

"Confronting ghosts."

"Good luck," he said with a smile.

As she drove down the driveway, Mike raised his hand in farewell, a mixture of concern and admiration filling his chest. He stood watching until her car disappeared, then closed his eyes briefly.

"Lord," he whispered into the morning air, "walk with her today. Help her find the peace she's looking for. And if I'm meant to be part of that peace, show us both the way forward."

Chapter 21

Abby drove with the windows down, letting the cool air whip through the car.

She pulled into a small gravel parking lot marked with a wooden sign: "New River Overlook & Picnic Area." She cut the engine and sat motionless, staring through the windshield.

This couldn't be right. Where rows of trailers had once stood, there was now an expansive grassy area dotted with picnic tables and charcoal grills. Where children had once played in dirt yards and adults had gathered on rickety porch steps, there were now hiking trail markers and interpretive signs about local wildlife.

This was definitely the place. Sunshine Acres Mobile Home Park had simply ceased to exist.

She stepped out of the car, the crunch of gravel under her shoes grounding her in the present moment. A light breeze carried the scent of pine and river water. In the distance, she could hear the rush of the New River as it carved its ancient path through the gorge.

Abby walked slowly across the grassy expanse, trying to overlay her fragmented memories onto this transformed landscape. That cluster of trees might have been close to where the community mailboxes stood. The slight rise in the land could have been where the manager's double-wide had dominated the entrance.

And somewhere, she turned in a slow circle. Somewhere around here had been trailer number 17, where she'd spent the first ten years of her life. Where she'd waited, hour after hour, for parents who never returned.

A hiking trail wound down toward the river, and Abby followed it, drawn by the sound of flowing water. The path descended through a stand of pine trees before opening onto a rocky shoreline where the New River spread wide and relatively calm. Several picnic tables were positioned to take advantage of the view.

Abby climbed onto the surface of one table, drawing her knees to her chest as she gazed out at the water. The river's surface danced with sunlight, flowing steadily eastward despite the rocks and fallen trees that occasionally disrupted its path.

The irony wasn't lost on her, that a place of such pain had been transformed into something beautiful. Nature and time had conspired to erase all physical evidence of Sunshine Acres Trailer Park, yet the emotional impact of what happened here had shaped every aspect of her life for twenty years.

Almost unconsciously, her fingers found the silver charm bracelet on her wrist. She'd put it on this morning, this tangible connection to a mother she barely remembered.

Had her mother loved to read? Had she loved to cook? Had her mother been a happy child? Did her father grow up in a loving family? How did her parents meet? Abby couldn't remember, or simply didn't know. The realization struck her like a physical blow. She knew very little about her parents. In her mind, they had become caricatures: the mother and father who abandoned her. She'd reduced them to that single defining action, never considering the complexity of their lives or the demons they battled.

"They were addicts," she said aloud, testing how the words felt in her mouth. "They had an illness."

A blue heron startled from the riverbank nearby, its enormous wings beating the air as it rose and glided downstream. Abby watched it go, envying the bird's freedom.

For so long, she'd told herself that leaving Laurel Ridge was about opportunity, about building a career worthy of her talents. But sitting here now, with the river flowing relentlessly before her, Abby recognized the deeper truth: she'd been running away. Running from pity, from whispers, from being "that poor Marshall girl." Running from the fear that she, too, might be unwanted, unworthy, disposable.

Charleston hadn't just been a career move; it had been an identity transplant. There, no one knew about the trailer park or the abandoned child. There, she could be simply Abigail Marshall, a rising star in interior design, sophisticated and self-sufficient.

"I built my entire life on what they did to me," she whispered to the river. "Every decision, every achievement... it was all about proving I was worth keeping."

The charm bracelet caught the sunlight, sending tiny reflections dancing across her jeans. Had her mother felt the same way once? Had she also tried to outrun some pain, only to find herself trapped in a cycle of addiction and desperation?

For the first time, Abby tried to imagine her parents not as the villains of her story, but as broken people fighting battles she couldn't see or understand. What kind of pain had driven them to choose drugs and alcohol over their child? What kind of despair had led them to that final, devastating choice?

"I spent twenty years hating you," she said to the empty air, imagining her words carrying downstream to wherever her parents might be, alive or dead, she might never know. "Twenty years letting that hate define me."

A tear slipped down her cheek, then another. She didn't bother wiping them away.

"I don't want to hate you anymore," she continued, voice breaking. "I don't even know you well enough to hate you. And I'm so tired of letting what you did determine who I am."

The quiet admission broke something loose inside her. Tears flowed freely, years of pent-up anger and hurt pouring out in heaving sobs that bent her double on the picnic table. She cried for the abandoned child she'd been, for the parents too consumed by addiction to stay, for the woman she'd become who measured her worth by accomplishments and acclaim.

When the storm of emotion finally subsided, Abby was exhausted but oddly lightened. She tilted her face to the sun, letting its warmth dry her tears.

"I need help," she admitted to herself. The revelation came without shame or self-judgment, just a clear recognition that her wounds ran deeper than she could heal alone. She would need to find a therapist, someone to guide her through unraveling twenty years of coping mechanisms and defense strategies.

The thought was both intimidating and liberating. She'd always prided herself on self-sufficiency, on needing no one. But perhaps true strength wasn't in standing alone, but in knowing when to reach for support.

Abby slipped off the picnic table and walked closer to the river's edge. The water lapped gently at the rocky shore, constantly in its forward motion. She knelt and dipped her fingers into the cool current, watching as it flowed around the obstacle of her hand without hesitation.

"I don't know how to pray about this," she said, the words feeling awkward but necessary. "I've spent so long being angry at You too, God. For letting them leave. For not making them better parents."

A fish jumped nearby, creating ripples that expanded outward in perfect circles.

"But I think I understand now that You didn't cause their addiction or their choices. And maybe... maybe You've been trying to help me heal all along. Through Aunt Gertrude and Uncle Wilburn. Through Leslie. Through Mike."

The name brought an unexpected warmth to her chest. Mike, with his quiet strength and steadfast kindness. Mike, who saw her, really saw her, and still looked at her with such tenderness.

"I don't know what You want for my life," Abby continued, her prayer gaining confidence. "Charleston or Laurel Ridge or somewhere else entirely. But I know I can't keep running. I can't keep letting my parents' actions dictate who I am."

She stood, brushing dirt from her knees. "Help me forgive them, Lord, because I need to be free of this. And help me see myself the way You see me, not as the girl whose parents left, but as someone worthy of love, just as I am."

As she spoke the last words, a profound sense of peace settled over her. Not the resolution of all her questions or the healing of all her wounds. That would take time and work, but a first step toward a different way of being.

Abby took one last look at the river before turning back toward the trail.

***

The drive back to Laurel Ridge felt different somehow. The landscape seemed more vibrant, the sky more expansive. Abby noticed details she'd missed on the outward journey: a field of wildflowers, an old barn with a faded advertisement painted on its side, a roadside stand selling local honey.

As she neared town, her phone rang through the car's Bluetooth system. Leslie's name appeared on the dashboard display.

"Hey," Abby answered, realizing she felt genuinely happy to hear from her friend.

"I've been trying to reach you for hours." Leslie's voice held a mix of relief and concern. "Are you okay? Mike mentioned you were taking some personal time today."

"I'm good," Abby said, surprised to find she meant it. "Better than I've been in a long time, actually. I went back to Sunshine Acres... or where it used to be."

"Oh, Abby." Leslie's tone softened. "That must have been intense."

"It was... necessary." Abby paused at a stop sign, then continued toward downtown. "I've been carrying this anger for so long, Leslie. It's defined everything: my career choices, my relationships, where I live."

"That's a heavy load to bear."

"Too heavy. I'm ready to put it down." Abby slowed as she entered the Laurel Ridge town limits. "I'm going to find a therapist. Someone to help me work through all of this."

"I think that's really brave," Leslie said. "And smart."

"I feel brave, believe it or not. It's a great feeling," Abby admitted. "I'm tired of being controlled by the past."

"You amaze me, Abby Marshall. You know I'll always be here for you if you need me."

Abby smiled, grateful for Leslie's unwavering support. "And I'm here for you if you ever need me to be. Listen, I'm pulling in the driveway at the house now. Talk more later?"

"Sounds good, my friend."

As she parked in the driveway, Abby was struck by the beauty of the house and the memories it held. This could be her home again, perhaps, if she chose to make it so.

The decision wasn't made yet. She still had much to consider, to pray about, to discuss with the therapist she would find. But Abby felt truly open to possibilities beyond her original plan.

She climbed the porch steps and paused to appreciate the late afternoon sunlight playing through the trees that surrounded her property.

Chapter 22

Abby sneezed as another cloud of dust billowed around her. The attic's stale air hung thick despite the two windows she'd managed to pry open at each end of the long space. Wiping her forehead with the back of her hand, she surveyed the intimidating landscape of boxes, trunks, and furniture draped in yellowed sheets that stretched before her.

In her mind's eye, she began to envision the space transformed, not as a storage area, but as a retreat. A sanctuary. The dormers could house window seats with plush cushions. Bookshelves could line the knee walls. A comfortable reading chair, perhaps a chaise lounge. No television, no computers. Just a place to think, to read, to be.

"A place to escape the noise of everyday life," she said aloud.

The idea startled her. She was planning to sell this house, not create a personal retreat area for herself. Yet here she was, thinking about a space she'd never be able to use.

Or would she?

Shaking the thought away, Abby turned to the task at hand. She needed to organize this mess before any renovation could happen, whether for herself or future owners. Methodically, she created three distinct areas: items to discard, items to donate, and things to keep.

An hour into her sorting, Abby's fingers brushed against a cardboard box tucked beneath an old dress form. Unlike the other boxes labeled with contents like "Christmas" or "Kitchen," this one bore two simple names written in Gertrude's elegant script: "Donna and Rick."

Her parents.

Abby's hands trembled as she pulled the box forward. It wasn't particularly large or heavy, just an ordinary cardboard banker's box.

She settled cross-legged on the dusty floor and lifted the lid. Inside, she found an assortment of things, none of which triggered any memories for her. A small crystal figurine of a bird, several paperback novels with cracked spines, and an empty woman's wallet worn smooth from use.

These must be things Gertrude had gathered from her parents' trailer. Things they hadn't considered worth taking when they fled.

Abby lifted out a small stuffed rabbit, its fur yellowed with age, one ear slightly torn.

"I don't remember you," she told the rabbit, turning it over in her hands. Had this been hers? Had her small hands clutched this rabbit for comfort when her parents were high or fighting?

Beneath the rabbit lay several children's books: *The Velveteen Rabbit*, *Goodnight Moon*, and a worn copy of *Where the Wild Things Are*. Abby opened the last one, finding childish scribbles on the inside cover and a note written in print she didn't recognize.

To Abby, on your 3rd birthday. Love, Mommy, and Daddy.

Something twisted in her chest. They had read to her once. They had celebrated her birthdays.

The next item made her breath catch. A baby quilt, hand-knitted in soft yellows and greens. She ran her fingers over the intricate pattern, imagining her mother, or perhaps Gertrude, creating it with love and anticipation for a baby not yet born.

"I wonder if you made this, Mom," she whispered, bringing the soft fabric to her cheek. It smelled of dust and attic, but she imagined she could detect a hint of the past, of baby powder and lullabies.

At the bottom of the box, Abby found what she both dreaded and longed for: a photo album. Her hands shook as she opened it.

The first photo showed a young woman with Abby's eyes and chin, holding her as a newborn. Her mother looked exhausted but radiant, gazing down at her with unmistakable love. Beside her stood a lanky man with a proud grin, his arm protectively around her mother's shoulders.

"Dad," Abby whispered, touching the image. Rick Marshall looked nothing like the haggard, desperate man of her few memories. Here, he was young, hopeful, and full of life.

She turned the pages slowly, watching herself grow from newborn to toddler. There she was, taking her first steps, her dad's hands hovering, ready to catch her. There she was on a tricycle, her mother kneeling beside her with a beaming smile. Birthday parties with homemade cakes. Christmas mornings with modest piles of presents.

A family. They had been a family once.

Then, around the age of five or six, the photos changed. They became fewer, the smiles more strained. In one, her mother looked noticeably thinner, dark circles under her eyes. In another, her dad's face had a hardness that hadn't been there before.

And then, nothing. No more photos documenting her growth beyond about age six. It was as if life had simply stopped being worth recording.

"This must have been when it started," Abby murmured, piecing together the visual evidence of her parents' descent into addiction. "When the drugs and alcohol began to take over."

She closed the album and held it against her chest, rocking slightly as tears welled in her eyes. The timeline was clear now: a young couple, possibly naïve but loving, and then their lives began crumbling as addiction took hold. Four or five years of struggle, of failing their daughter in increasingly serious ways, until finally, they disappeared into their addiction altogether.

Abby leaned back against a trunk, letting the tears flow. She wasn't crying for the loss of her parents, she'd done that years ago. She was crying for the waste of it all. The sheer, tragic waste.

"You missed everything," she said aloud. "You missed my first day of middle school. You missed when I won the art contest in ninth grade. You missed my proms, my graduation from high school. College. My first apartment. My first big design job."

Her voice grew stronger, infused not with anger but with a profound sadness.

"You missed watching your only child grow up. And for what? For drugs? Was it worth it?"

The question hung in the dusty air, unanswerable. Abby closed her eyes, letting a new awareness wash over her. All these years, she'd carried the weight of being abandoned, wearing it like a badge of both shame and defiance. But now, sitting amidst the remnants of what once was, she saw the situation with painful clarity.

Her parents hadn't just abandoned her, they'd abandoned themselves. They'd abandoned any chance of watching their daughter grow into the woman she became. They'd abandoned sunrises and birthdays, laughter and tears, all the beauty and pain that made up a fully lived life.

And if it hadn't been for the grace of God, she might have followed their path.

The realization hit her with startling force. If her parents hadn't left. If Gertrude and Wilburn hadn't taken her in, if they hadn't provided stability and love, who knows what might have happened? She could have ended up in foster care, bounced from home to home. She could have developed her own addictions, seeking escape from pain, just as her parents had.

"Thank you," she whispered, the words directed both to her aunt and uncle and to God. "Thank you for saving me from that."

She gathered the photo album, the knitted blanket, and the stuffed rabbit, leaving the rest of the items in the box. These pieces of her past, these tangible reminders of a time before... these she would keep. Not to dwell on what was lost, but to acknowledge where she had come from and how far she had traveled.

The anger that had been her companion for so long was becoming quieter, more reflective. Her parents' story was tragic, but it wasn't hers. She had been given a different path. She had been given a choice.

The attic suddenly felt too confined for the emotions swirling within her. She needed air, perspective, someone to talk to. Abby headed for the attic stairs.

Chapter 23

Abby stepped through the front door, balancing a cardboard tray with two coffee cups in one hand and a paper bag of muffins in the other. The sound of a radio playing soft country music drifted from the kitchen, along with the occasional scrape of a drywall knife against plaster. A smile tugged at her lips as she walked toward the noise, careful to avoid the tarps and tools scattered across the floor.

"Mike?" she called, rounding the corner into what was becoming her new kitchen.

He was balanced on a stepladder, his back to her, as he smoothed the joint compound over a seam in the drywall. His T-shirt stretched across his shoulders as he worked, dust clinging to the fabric and speckling his dark hair.

Mike glanced over his shoulder, his face lighting up when he saw her. "Hey," he said, setting his trowel on the top step of the ladder. "I thought you were taking the day off."

"I was, and I am, but I thought you might need caffeine reinforcements," she lifted the coffee tray. "And Martha had fresh blueberry muffins."

"You're a lifesaver." Mike climbed down from the ladder, wiping his hands on a rag tucked into his back pocket.

Abby handed him a coffee cup and set the bag of muffins on the makeshift table of plywood and sawhorses.

He took a sip of coffee. His eyes crinkled at the corners when he smiled at her over the rim of the cup. "Perfect. Thank you."

"You're welcome. The kitchen's really coming together, isn't it?"

Mike nodded, reaching for a muffin. "The plumber said he can install the sink and dishwasher next Tuesday after the cabinets are installed."

"And the wall here?" Abby walked to where the old dividing wall between the kitchen and dining room had been. Now the space flowed openly, making the whole area feel larger and more inviting. "I'm really glad that wall is gone. It changes everything."

"It does." Mike followed her, standing close enough that she could smell the clean scent of his cologne. "Makes the space feel more like you."

"Like me?" She turned to look up at him, curious.

"Open. Welcoming. Not closed off."

Abby felt her cheeks warm slightly.

"I haven't always been so open. I see that now," she admitted, taking a sip of her coffee to collect her thoughts. "Charleston Abby, was all about maintaining perfect boundaries."

"And Laurel Ridge, Abby?" Mike asked, his hazel eyes steady on hers.

"Still figuring that out." She paused before continuing. "I was in the attic earlier and found a box of my parents' things." The words came out in a rush. "Photos, books, my baby blanket, things I don't even remember. And I just... I need to talk to someone."

"Let's go for a walk," he suggested. "You look like you could use some fresh air."

Outside, the air carried the crisp scent of late spring as they headed toward the small park a block away. Mike walked close beside her, waiting for her to speak.

"I saw my whole childhood in photos today," Abby finally said as they reached the park's wrought-iron entrance. "At least, the early part of it. My parents holding me as a baby, birthdays, Christmases... they looked so normal, Mike. So happy."

They found an empty bench beneath a maple tree. As they sat, Mike turned slightly toward her, giving her his full attention.

"And then around the time I was five or six, the photos just... changed. I could literally see my parents changing in the pictures... getting thinner, looking stressed, the light going out of their eyes."

"That must have been when their addiction was taking hold," Mike said.

Abby nodded, wrapping her arms around herself against a chill that had nothing to do with the temperature. "It made everything so real in a way it hasn't been before. They weren't just 'the parents who abandoned me.' They were people who had dreams once, who loved their baby, who read me bedtime stories. And then they lost it all—including me."

She paused for a few seconds and gathered her thoughts before continuing. "The worst part is realizing how much they missed. Not just raising me, but living. Really living. They traded everything... watching their daughter grow up, holidays, ordinary Tuesdays... for drugs." Her voice cracked. "What a waste. What an absolute waste of life."

Mike was quiet for a moment, considering her words. "That's a powerful realization," he finally said. "Most people in your position would only see how they were hurt personally by someone's actions. You are choosing to see how your parents hurt themselves, too."

"I just keep thinking that could have been me," Abby admitted, meeting his eyes. "If Aunt Gertrude and Uncle Wilburn hadn't taken me in, if I'd gone into foster care or if my parents had stayed... who knows what path I might have taken? Addiction can be genetic. I could have followed in their footsteps."

"But you didn't," Mike reminded her gently. "You built a beautiful life."

"Because God put people in my life who loved me when my parents couldn't." Abby looked down at her hands. "I've been so angry for so long, Mike. Angry at them for leaving, angry at myself for not being enough to make them stay. But today, looking at those photos, all I felt was sad. Just... profoundly sad for all of us."

Mike hesitated, then carefully took her hand in his. His palm was warm and slightly rough against her skin. "That sounds like the beginning of forgiveness to me."

"Maybe it is. I don't know if I'll ever understand why they left, but I accept that it wasn't about me. It was about their illness, their addiction. They lost themselves before they ever lost me."

They sat in companionable silence for several minutes, her hand still in his. The park was quiet in the late afternoon, just a few dog walkers and joggers passing by.

"Thank you," Abby said eventually. "For dropping everything and listening to me when I needed a friend."

Mike squeezed her hand gently. "Always."

That single word, spoken with such quiet certainty, sent warmth spreading through her chest. She looked at him, really looked at him, taking in the steadiness of his gaze, the strength in his shoulders, the genuine concern in his expression.

"Mike Hatfield," she said slowly, "I think you might be the most dependable man I've known."

A faint blush colored his cheeks. "Is that a good thing or a boring thing?"

"It's a rare thing," she replied honestly. "And I think rare is exactly what I need."

His eyes widened slightly at the implication behind her words.

Abby's stomach growled loudly, breaking the moment.

Mike laughed. "When's the last time you ate?"

Abby thought back through her day. "Um... coffee counts as breakfast, right?"

"Absolutely not." He stood, still holding her hand, and gently pulled her to her feet. "Come on. Martha made chicken pot pies today."

"How do you know that?"

"Small town," he replied with a smile. "I have my sources."

As they walked toward the diner, their hands still linked, Abby felt a peculiar lightness. The discoveries in the attic had been painful, but somehow, they had lifted a burden rather than adding one.

"You know," she said as they approached Martha's, "I think I might have figured out what to do with the attic space."

"Oh?" Mike held the diner door open for her.

"A reading retreat. A quiet space. Window seats in the dormers, bookshelves along the knee walls, maybe a chaise lounge. Somewhere peaceful to escape to without actually escaping."

The significance of her words wasn't lost on Mike. His eyes searched hers. "Sounds perfect," he said. "For whoever ends up living there."

Martha greeted them with raised eyebrows and a knowing smile as they slid into a booth. "Well, well. To what do I owe the pleasure?"

"Oh, we were just in the mood for your chicken pot pie," Mike answered with a grin. "If there's any left."

"For you two? I'll make sure of it." Martha winked at Abby. "Coffee while you wait?"

"Please," Abby nodded gratefully.

As Martha bustled away, Mike leaned forward. "Are you really okay? It's been an emotional day for you."

Abby considered the question seriously. "I am, actually. Better than what I've been in what feels like forever. It's like... I've been carrying this heavy backpack of anger for years, and today I finally set it down. I'm sad about my parents... I most likely always will be... but I don't feel defined by what they did anymore. I don't know how to explain it, I just feel different. Like I'm seeing things differently now... like the clouds have gone away, and all there is are clear blue skies and a bright shiny sun."

"That's huge, Abby."

"It feels huge," she agreed. "And a little scary. If I'm not the abandoned daughter fighting to prove herself anymore, who am I?"

Mike's eyes were warm as they held hers. "You're Abby Marshall. Talented designer. Kind-hearted friend. A brave woman who faces her past instead of running from it. That's who you are."

Martha returned with coffee. "Two pot pies coming right up," she announced, filling their mugs. "You two want a slice of blueberry pie for dessert? Just came out of the oven."

"Yes, please," they answered simultaneously, then laughed.

After Martha left, Abby stirred cream into her coffee, gathering her thoughts. "There's something else I realized today," she said.

"What's that?"

"I've been so focused on what I lost when my parents left that I never fully appreciated what I gained with Gertrude and Wilburn." She wrapped her hands around the warm mug. "They saved my life, Mike. Not just by taking me in, but by loving me so completely. They created this... this sanctuary for me."

"They were pretty amazing people," Mike said. "Everyone in town respected them."

"And now I understand why Aunt Gertrude spent all those years trying to track down my parents. It wasn't to confront them or punish them. It was mercy, plain and simple... she was trying to find them, trying to reach out, trying to help them... trying to give them a chance to know the daughter they left behind."

"She was fierce about protecting the people she loved."

"I wish I'd known sooner. About her search, about my parents' addiction. I spent so many years thinking they just didn't want me, that I wasn't enough. When, really, they were sick. They needed help they never got."

Martha arrived with two steaming pot pies, the buttery crust golden and flaky. "Eat up while it's hot," she instructed, sliding the plates in front of them. "Can I get you anything else?"

"This looks perfect, thank you," Abby smiled gratefully.

As they ate, the conversation shifted to lighter topics, the progress on the house, Tyler's upcoming science project, the summer festival the church was planning. It felt normal, comfortable. Like they'd been having dinner together for years rather than weeks.

"Tyler's been asking when he can see the house again," Mike mentioned as they started on their blueberry pie. "He's got it in his head that he needs to check on the 'round room' progress."

Abby laughed. "The turret room... I haven't even started in there yet, but he's welcome anytime. Maybe this weekend?"

"He'd love that." Mike hesitated, then added, "I was thinking... there's a movie night in the town square this Friday. They're showing 'Back to the Future' on a big screen. Tyler's staying at his friend's house, so I thought maybe..."

"Are you asking me on a date, Mike Hatfield?" Abby couldn't help the smile spreading across her face.

"I am," he confirmed, a touch of his usual shyness returning.

"I'd love to," she said.

His face lit up with a smile that made her heart flutter. "Great. That's... great."

"Very articulate," she teased.

"You make me nervous sometimes," he admitted with a self-deprecating laugh.

"Me? Why?"

Mike set down his fork, his expression suddenly serious. "Because this matters, Abby. You matter. I've spent eight years focusing on Tyler and work, convincing myself that was enough. And then you came back to town and..." He paused, searching for the right words. "It's like I remembered there's this whole other part of life I've been missing."

The honesty in his voice touched something deep within her. "I know exactly what you mean," she said. "I've been so focused on my career, on proving myself, that I forgot what it feels like to just... connect with someone. I think it's time we both start living again. Really living and enjoying everything God has given us."

Their eyes held across the table, the moment stretching between them, full of promise and possibility.

Chapter 24

Mike parked his truck in front of Abby's house the next morning, grabbing his thermos of coffee and work bag.

The front door opened before he reached the porch, and Abby stood there in a simple t-shirt and jeans, her hair pulled back in a casual ponytail. Something about her seemed different this morning, a softness in her eyes, perhaps, and no hesitation in her smile.

"Good Morning," she said, holding the door open. "I was hoping to catch you before you got started in the kitchen."

Mike raised an eyebrow as he stepped inside. "Everything okay? Did we hit a snag or something?"

"No, nothing like that." She closed the door behind him. "The kitchen plans are perfect. I just..." She paused, tucking a loose strand of hair behind her ear. "I was wondering if you could come upstairs with me for a bit. To the turret room."

Mike set his things down by the door. "Sure. Let me just text the guys to let them know I'll be starting a little later in the kitchen, and they can go ahead with our plans for the day."

As he sent a quick message to his crew, he noticed Abby fidgeting with the hem of her shirt, something he'd never seen her do before.

"Lead the way," he said, pocketing his phone.

The turret room stood at the end of the upstairs hallway on the third floor, its rounded walls creating an almost magical space that had always been one of his favorite architectural features of the Marshall house. The room was untouched by renovation so far.

"I've been thinking about this space," Abby said, stepping into the center of the circular room. "It was always one of my favorite spots in the house when I was growing up."

Mike leaned against the door frame, watching her. "I remember. You mentioned that during Tyler's tour."

"I was hoping..." She turned to face him fully. "Would you mind helping me think through some ideas for this room? I know it wasn't on our immediate schedule, but—"

"I'd be happy to," Mike interrupted, sensing her uncharacteristic uncertainty. "This is your project, Abby. If you want to focus on the turret room today, that's what we'll do."

Relief washed over her face. "Thank you. I brought some cushions up earlier." She gestured to a few large floor pillows she'd placed by the windows. "I thought we could sit and brainstorm."

Mike crossed the room and settled onto one of the cushions, and Abby sat across from him.

"So, what are you thinking about this space?" he asked.

Abby took a deep breath, her eyes traveling around the room. "That's just it. I've been thinking about a lot more than just this room."

Mike waited, sensing she needed space to find her words.

"When I first came back to Laurel Ridge, this house was simply a renovation project to me," she continued. "A stepping stone to get back to Charleston and restart my career there. But now..." She met his eyes. "Now I'm seriously considering staying here."

Mike forced himself to remain still, to not reveal how his heart had quickened at her admission.

"Staying," he repeated carefully.

Abby nodded. "It feels right. These past weeks, working on this house, reconnecting with everyone... with you..." Her cheeks colored slightly.

Mike leaned forward slightly. "What would staying look like for you?"

"I'd live here," she said. "Not sell it after all. And I'd start my design business here—a home-based business, maybe with a small studio space downtown, eventually."

"You think Laurel Ridge has enough demand for an interior designer?" Mike asked, not to discourage her, but to understand how thoroughly she'd considered this.

"I do, actually. Between here and the surrounding towns, there's more potential than I initially thought. Martha mentioned that people from surrounding towns and cities often come to Laurel Ridge for services. Plus, I could take on some clients in large cities that may be a little further away... maybe commute once or twice a month for meetings."

"Sounds like you've been doing your homework."

"I have," she admitted. "But it's more than just business calculations. Being back here has made me realize how empty my life in Charleston was. I had a successful career, but nothing else. No real friends, no community..." She hesitated. "No one to come home to at night."

The vulnerability in her voice made his chest tighten. "And you think you could find those things here in Laurel Ridge?"

"I think I already have." Her voice was soft, but her eyes held his steadily.

Mike swallowed hard, fighting the hope rising in his chest. "What about this room, then?" he asked, gesturing to the turret space around them. "If you're staying, what would you want to do with it?"

A smile spread across Abby's face, lighting up her eyes. "I've been thinking about that. When I was a kid, this was my reading nook. Aunt Gertrude had, at one time, a couple of recliners in here and a sofa, and I'd spend hours here with books." She looked up at the ceiling. "But I'm thinking now it could be a private design space... kind of like a home office."

Mike could see it immediately. Abby working at a beautiful desk, sketching designs, the light from the curved windows illuminating her face.

"It would be perfect," he said. "We could build custom shelving along these interior walls, and a large desk for you to work at. And the floors in here are in good condition. We'd just need to refinish them."

Abby's eyes lit up as he spoke. "Yes! And I'd want to keep the historical character intact while making it functional." She scooted closer, her knees now touching his as she gestured enthusiastically. "The paint color would be important too, something warm but neutral, to make the woodwork stand out."

For several minutes, they exchanged ideas about the space, their conversation flowing easily from practical considerations to design aesthetics. Mike found himself caught up in her enthusiasm, their professional rapport enhanced by the personal connection that had been building between them.

Eventually, the conversation lulled, and Abby looked down at her hands.

"There's something else I wanted to talk to you about," she said.

"What's that?"

She looked up, meeting his eyes directly. "Where do you see yourself in the future, Mike? I mean..." She took a deep breath. "You and me. Do you think we could have a future?"

The directness of her question caught him off guard. He'd been thinking about this very thing for days now, imagining what it might be like to build a life with Abby, to bring her into his and Tyler's world permanently. But hearing her ask it outright made his carefully considered thoughts scatter like leaves in the wind.

"I—" He paused, wanting to give her an honest answer but struggling to find the right words. "Abby, I've thought about that more than you know."

Her face fell slightly at his hesitation, and he quickly reached for her hand.

"No, listen," he said. "I'm not hesitating because I don't see a future for us. I'm just trying to say this right." He squeezed her hand gently. "What's growing between us is deep. I'm not sure how to explain it, but I have feelings for you, and you've made an impression on me. I do see a future with you—one I want very much. But I need to be careful, not just for my sake, but for Tyler's."

Abby nodded, understanding in her eyes. "Of course. Tyler comes first."

"It's not just that," Mike continued. "After Cora died, I closed that part of my heart off. I focused on being a dad and building my business. The idea of letting someone in again, of risking that kind of loss..." He shook his head. "It scares me. But being with you these past weeks has made me want to take that risk again."

"I understand risk aversion better than most people," she said. "Can I tell you something I've never told anyone else?"

"Anything," Mike replied, still holding her hand.

"I've never been in a real relationship," she confessed. "Ever. I mean, I've been on dates, but never beyond a first date. I never let anyone get close enough."

Mike couldn't hide his surprise. "Never? But you're so…" He gestured vaguely with his free hand. "I mean, you're beautiful, successful, kind. I assumed you'd have men lining up in Charleston."

Abby laughed, but there was a touch of sadness in it. "I decided long ago it was safer to be alone. I convinced myself that I wanted to spend my life focused on my career, never depending on anyone else." She looked down at their joined hands. "I realize now how much I've missed out on because of that decision."

"We've both been hiding from something," Mike said quietly.

"Fear of abandonment for me, fear of loss for you," Abby agreed. "Not the healthiest starting point for a relationship."

"Maybe not," Mike said. "But at least we're honest about it. We both understand what it means to protect your heart, but we're both willing to try, anyway."

Abby smiled, a genuine smile that reached her eyes. "I'd like that. To try, I mean. With you."

Mike felt his heart expand in his chest, a warmth spreading through him that had nothing to do with the morning sun filling the room.

The shrill ring of a cell phone shattered the moment.

Abby jerked back, her hand flying to her pocket. "I'm so sorry," she said, looking flustered. "I should have put it on silent." She glanced at the screen. "It's a Charleston area code. Probably a sales call, but…"

"Go ahead and answer," Mike said, trying to hide his disappointment at the interrupted moment.

Abby hesitated, then hit the answer button. "Hello, this is Abby Marshall."

Mike watched as her expression shifted from mild annoyance to surprise, then to unmistakable excitement.

"Mrs. Saunders! Yes, of course I remember you." She straightened up, her professional demeanor sliding into place like a well-worn glove. "How are you?"

As the conversation continued, Mike could hear only Abby's side, but it was enough to piece together what was happening. The Saunders, apparently former clients from her Charleston days, had purchased a home on Folly Island and wanted Abby to take on the interior design work.

"That's a beautiful property," Abby was saying, her voice animated. "When did you close on it?"

Mike leaned back against the wall, watching the excitement build in Abby's eyes as she listened to the details of the project. He'd seen this side of her before, the passionate designer in her element, lighting up at the possibility of a creative challenge.

"A complete redesign of the entire house? That would be…" She glanced at Mike, then away. "That would certainly be an extensive project."

Another pause as she listened.

"Yes, I am currently out of town, working on a renovation, but—" She stopped mid-sentence, listening again.

"That's extremely generous, Mrs. Saunders." Her eyebrows raised. "And you'd need me to start next month?"

Mike felt a knot forming in his stomach. He could see where this was going, could see the pull of opportunity tugging at Abby even as she'd just finished talking about staying in Laurel Ridge.

"Could I call you back tomorrow? I'd like to think about the logistics." She nodded. "Yes, I have your number. Thank you so much for thinking of me. I'm truly flattered."

She ended the call and stared at the phone in her hand for a moment before looking up at Mike.

"That was Katherine Saunders," she said, her voice slightly breathless. "She and her husband were clients at Reed Interiors. They just purchased a historic home on Folly Island, right on the beach. They want me to handle the entire redesign."

"Sounds like a big opportunity," Mike said carefully, trying to keep his voice neutral despite the sinking feeling in his chest.

"It is," Abby agreed. "They're offering double my usual rate, plus a completion bonus. It would probably be a six-month project, minimum." Her eyes were bright with professional excitement, but he could see conflict there too. "It's exactly the kind of prestigious project that could launch my independent career."

Mike nodded slowly. "In Charleston, South Carolina."

"Yes." She looked down at her hands. "In Charleston."

The silence that fell between them felt heavy with unspoken thoughts. Just minutes ago, they'd been talking about a future together in Laurel Ridge. Now, South Carolina was calling Abby back.

"When would you need to leave?" Mike asked, his voice sounding strangely formal to his own ears.

"They want to start next month," Abby replied. "But I haven't accepted yet. I told her I needed to think about it."

"Of course." Mike nodded, struggling to keep his emotions in check. "It's a big decision."

"Mike," Abby said, reaching for his hand again. "Ten minutes ago, I was telling you I wanted to stay in Laurel Ridge. That hasn't changed just because of one phone call."

"Hasn't it?" he asked, more sharply than he intended. "Abby, I saw your face when you were on the phone. You lit up like a Christmas tree. It's clearly something you want to do."

"Yes, professionally, it's an amazing opportunity," she admitted. "But that doesn't mean it's the right choice for me personally."

Mike stood up, needing to put some physical distance between them as he processed his thoughts. "I don't want to be the reason you turn down something that could be so important for your career."

Abby rose to her feet as well, her expression troubled. "You're not the only factor in my decision, Mike. It's about what I want my life to look like. What will make me truly happy?"

"And what is that?" he asked, his voice low. "Because from where I'm standing, it seems like you were pretty happy about this new Charleston job."

"Of course, I was excited," she said. "It's a fantastic opportunity in my field. But being excited about a job offer doesn't mean I'm ready to pack up my car and head out." She stepped closer to him.

Mike wanted to believe her, wanted to trust that what was growing between them was strong enough to withstand the pull of her career ambitions. But years of protecting his heart made caution his default.

"I think you should take some time to really think about what you want," he said. "No rush decisions. This is your career we're talking about, Abby. Your future."

"And what about our future?"

Mike felt his resolve wavering at the vulnerability in her eyes. "I'm not going anywhere," he said. "Laurel Ridge is my home. It's where I'm raising my son. It's where I want to be. But you..." He took a deep breath. "You need to figure out where you want to be."

"I already told you," she said, a hint of frustration in her voice. "I'm thinking of staying here, in this house, in Laurel Ridge."

"And now you have another option to consider," he said gently. "One that might align better with the career you've worked so hard to build."

Abby pressed her lips together, studying his face. "You're pulling away," she said. "I can feel it. You're putting distance between us."

Mike ran a hand through his hair. "I'm being realistic," he countered. "You talk about staying, about building something here, and then with one phone call... Charleston seems to be pulling you back. You left once before..."

"That's not fair," she said, her voice tight. "I was eighteen when I left for college. This is different."

"Is it?" Mike asked. "Because from where I'm standing, it looks pretty similar. An exciting opportunity in Charleston versus the quiet life in Laurel Ridge. And I'm not convinced you're ready to choose the latter."

Abby took a step back, hurt flashing in her eyes. "You don't get to decide what I'm ready for, Mike. And if you're already assuming I'll leave, then maybe you're not as serious about this thing that is growing between us as I thought you might be."

The accusation stung, all the more because Mike knew it was his fear talking—fear of opening his heart fully only to watch her walk away.

"That's not it," he said. "I'm very serious, Abby. That's why this is so hard."

She crossed her arms over her chest. "Then why are you pushing me away before I've even made a decision?"

"Because I have to protect myself," he admitted. "And more importantly, I have to protect Tyler. He's already getting attached to you. If you leave..." He shook his head. "I can't set him up for that kind of disappointment."

Abby's expression softened. "I understand that. I do. But you're assuming I'll choose Charleston, and that's not fair to either of us."

Mike studied her face, trying to read her true feelings. "What are you going to do, then?"

"I'm going to think about it," she said. "Really think about what I want my life to look like. Where I want to be, and who I would like to be with." She stepped closer to him again. "But I need you to believe that I'm seriously considering staying here. That this isn't just a passing notion for me."

Mike wanted to believe her. He wanted it more than he'd wanted anything in a long time. But the fear of loss that had been his constant companion since Cora died wasn't so easily dismissed.

"I'll do my best," he said finally. "That's all I can promise right now."

Abby nodded, disappointment evident in her eyes but acceptance there too. "I suppose that's fair."

An awkward silence fell between them, the intimate atmosphere of earlier completely dissolved. Mike glanced at his watch.

"I should probably get downstairs," he said.

"Of course," Abby said, her professional mask sliding back into place. "We've got work to do."

As Mike turned to leave the turret room, he paused at the doorway, looking back at Abby standing in the center of the circular space, morning light surrounding her. She looked both vulnerable and strong, uncertain and determined, all at once.

"For what it's worth," he said, "I hope you stay."

A small smile touched her lips. "For what it's worth, I hope I stay, too."

Mike nodded and headed downstairs, his mind swirling with conflicting emotions.

As he rejoined his crew in the kitchen, watching them sanding the drywall and going through the motions of measuring and marking cabinet placements, Mike found himself sending up a silent prayer.

Lord, give her clarity. And give me the strength to accept whatever she decides.

The sounds of construction filled the house, but upstairs in the turret room, Abby remained alone with her thoughts, caught between two possible futures, and both were filled with promise in different ways. The choice was entirely hers to make.

Chapter 25

Abby pushed open the door to Leslie's Blossoms. The sweet fragrance of fresh flowers enveloped her immediately, offering momentary relief from the turmoil in her mind. She spotted Leslie at the counter, her auburn hair tied back in a loose braid, arranging pink roses and baby's breath in a clear glass vase.

"Hey," Abby called, her voice betraying more emotion than she'd intended.

Leslie looked up, her hands pausing mid-arrangement. Her eyes narrowed slightly as she studied Abby's face. "What's wrong?"

"Is it that obvious?" Abby asked, attempting a smile that didn't quite reach her eyes.

"Yes." Leslie finished placing the last stem into the arrangement and wiped her hands on her green apron.

Without another word, Leslie walked to the front door, flipped the lock, and turned the hanging sign to "Out to Lunch." She returned to the counter, removed her apron, and placed her hands on her hips.

"Tea or coffee?" she asked.

"Tea, please," Abby replied, her shoulders sagging slightly with relief. She hadn't realized how much she needed this—someone who would drop everything to listen without her having to explain why.

Leslie gestured upstairs. "Come on. I've got chamomile and Earl Grey up there."

Abby followed Leslie up the narrow staircase that led to her apartment. The space was cozy and bright, filled with potted plants and colorful throw pillows. Leslie's style was eclectic, but comfortable, much like the woman herself.

"Make yourself at home," Leslie said, filling a kettle with water and placing it on the stove. "I'm guessing this is about Mike?"

Abby sank into the small sofa by the window, tucking her feet beneath her. "Partly. But it's more than that. It's... everything." She watched as Leslie moved efficiently around the kitchen, pulling mugs from a cabinet and tea bags from a decorative tin.

"Start wherever you want," Leslie said. "I'm all ears."

Abby took a deep breath. "I got a call from Charleston this morning."

Leslie paused, turning to face her. "Oh? What kind of call?"

"A job offer. A really good one, actually." Abby twisted her fingers together in her lap. "The Saunders... the clients I lost when the firm went bankrupt. They want to hire me directly. They're offering me a contract for a historic home renovation, with a substantial fee plus a bonus, if I can complete it by their deadline."

"Wow." Leslie leaned against the counter, her expression carefully neutral. "That sounds like exactly what you need to boost your new business."

"It is. Or it should be." Abby shook her head. "That's the problem. It's the perfect opportunity, and I... I don't want it."

The kettle began to whistle, and Leslie turned to pour the hot water into two mugs. She carried them over to the coffee table in front of Abby, setting them down before taking a seat in the armchair opposite.

"You don't want it."

"Am I crazy?" Abby asked, looking up at her friend with genuine confusion. "Would I be completely insane to say no? Just like that? No questions asked? No second thoughts?"

Leslie blew gently on her tea. "That depends. Why don't you want it?"

Abby wrapped her hands around the warm mug, grateful for its solidity when everything else felt so uncertain. "I've been sitting with this decision all morning, trying to make a pros and cons list in my head. The Charleston job is everything I thought I wanted—prestige, good money, high-end clients, creative freedom. But..." She trailed off.

"It doesn't feel right," Leslie finished for her.

"No, it doesn't." Abby took a small sip of her tea. "And it's not just about Mike, though he's definitely part of it. It's the house. I started out renovating it to sell, but now I can't imagine someone else living there. It's about this town, and the people, and this sense of... feeling like I belong here. I want to be here."

Leslie smiled softly. "That's not crazy, Abby. That's called finding your home."

"But I've worked so hard to establish myself in my career, to become someone." Abby's voice caught slightly. "What if I'm just running away from challenges again? What if I'm making this decision based on emotions rather than logic?"

"Since when is choosing happiness illogical? Besides, your career isn't ending if you stay here. It's just changing direction."

Abby nodded slowly. "I've been thinking about that, too. There's a need for it here, not just high-end renovations, but helping regular people make their spaces beautiful and functional. I could do consultations for folks who can't afford full design services, maybe teach some workshops at the community center."

"I think that sounds amazing," Leslie said, her eyes lighting up.

"And I'd be close to people who matter to me." Abby set her mug down and leaned forward. "I've spent so much of my life trying to prove something. But what if I don't have anything to prove anymore? What if I can just... be?"

Leslie reached across and squeezed Abby's hand. "That's called freedom, sweetie."

"It's scary," Abby admitted. "Starting over again at thirty."

"Is it starting over, though? Or is it picking up where you left off, just with more wisdom and experience?"

Abby considered this. "Maybe you're right. Maybe this is where I was always meant to end up, and Charleston was just a detour I needed to take."

"So what are you going to tell the Saunders?" Leslie asked after a moment.

"I'm going to thank them for the opportunity and decline."

"And what about Mike?" Leslie asked, a small smile playing at her lips.

"I'd be lying if I said he wasn't a major factor in me wanting to stay here."

"He's a good man," Leslie said simply.

"He is. It's strange how quickly he's become important to me."

"Not strange at all," Leslie countered. "When something's right, you know it. Sometimes it takes time, and sometimes it hits you all at once."

Abby sipped her tea thoughtfully. "There's another piece to all this. I've been thinking a lot about my parents."

Leslie nodded encouragingly.

"I've spent most of my life being angry at them, using that anger as fuel to prove I could succeed without them. But now..." Abby paused, gathering her thoughts. "Now I understand that they were just broken people who made terrible choices. It doesn't excuse what they did, but holding on to that anger is only hurting me."

"That's a powerful."

"I've been praying about it," Abby admitted. "Really praying, not just going through the motions. And I'm starting to feel this... release. Like forgiving them isn't about saying what they did was okay, but about freeing myself from being defined by their actions."

Leslie's eyes shone with unshed tears. "I'm so proud of you, Abby. I don't think you realize how much you've grown since you came back."

"I don't think I would have gotten here without coming back to Laurel Ridge," Abby said. "Without reconnecting more with you, with the church, with this community. Without meeting Mike."

"God works in mysterious ways," Leslie said with a small smile.

"He certainly does."

"So, what's your next step?" Leslie asked.

"First, I need to call the Saunders and gracefully decline their offer," Abby said, straightening her shoulders with newfound resolve. "Then I need to start making concrete plans."

"What about the house?" Leslie asked.

"I'll be renovating it to live in, not to sell." Abby smiled. "I can take more time with it, make it exactly what I want rather than what would appeal to potential buyers."

"And what about Mike? Are you going to tell him you're staying?"

Abby hesitated. "Yes, but I also don't want him to think my decision is solely because of him. I need to be certain I'm staying for the right reasons—for myself first."

Leslie nodded. "That makes sense. He deserves to know where things stand."

"He does," Abby acknowledged. "Thanks for this. For locking your door and making time for me. For listening without judging."

"That's what friends are for," Leslie replied with a warm smile. "Especially friends who've known each other since we were stealing each other's crayons in kindergarten."

Abby laughed. "I'd forgotten about that. You always took the blue ones."

"Because blue is clearly the superior crayon color," Leslie said with mock seriousness, then grinned. "I'm here for you. Whatever you decide and however it works out. But honestly... I think you already have it all figured out."

"I believe I do. I feel like I'm in a good place."

Leslie leaned forward, suddenly business-like. "So, practical matters. If you're starting a design business here, you'll need a name, business cards, a website..."

Abby smiled at her friend's enthusiasm. "What do you think of 'Marshall Designs' as the name? Simple, clean, and it honors Aunt Gertrude and Uncle Wilburn."

"It's perfect," Leslie declared. "And we could have a launch party at the house once the renovations are complete. Show off your work and announce your new business to the town at the same time."

"That's a great idea," Abby said, her mind already spinning with possibilities. "I could set up a portfolio room in the house, maybe use one of the spare bedrooms as a consultation space."

"See? You're already thinking like a business owner," Leslie said with satisfaction. "This will be amazing, Abby. I just know it."

"It feels right, in a way that nothing has for a long time."

Leslie checked her watch and sighed. "I should probably head back downstairs soon. Mrs. Peterson is coming to pick up that arrangement at one."

"Of course," Abby said, standing up. "I've monopolized enough of your time."

"Nonsense," Leslie waved dismissively. "This was important. Besides, listening to your life-changing epiphanies is way more interesting than anything else."

Abby laughed and gathered her purse. "Thanks again, Les. For everything."

"Just promise me one thing," Leslie said as they headed toward the stairs.

"What's that?"

"When you and Mike get married... and you will, mark my word... I get to be maid of honor at the wedding."

Abby felt her cheeks flush crimson. "Let's not get ahead of ourselves."

"Details, details," Leslie said with a wink. "I'm just saying, I've got dibs."

Chapter 26

The house hummed with activity as Abby opened the front door, the persistent rhythm of hammers, the whine of an electric saw from somewhere in the back, and the murmur of voices carrying through the open spaces.

"Hello?" she called out.

Frank poked his head around the corner from the dining room. "Hey there, Ms. Marshall."

"Frank, I've told you a dozen times to call me Abby," she said with a smile.

"Old habits." He shrugged good-naturedly. "Need something?"

"Actually, I was looking for Mike."

"Boss man's upstairs in the turret room. He's been up there for about an hour now."

Abby's curiosity piqued. "The turret room?"

"I have no idea. He headed up there with a notepad and measuring tape." Frank winked and returned to his work, leaving Abby staring at the staircase.

She climbed the steps, her hand trailing along the smooth banister that had just been refinished.

Abby paused in the doorway of the room, taking in the scene before her. Mike stood with his back to her, a measuring tape extended across one of the curved walls. Sunlight filtered through the windows. His simple gray t-shirt stretched across his shoulders as he reached up to mark something on the wall. A notepad lay open on a small folding table he must have brought up.

She watched him work. This was the man who had somehow, against all her carefully constructed defenses, found his way into her heart.

Mike must have sensed her presence because he suddenly stilled, then turned. Their eyes met, and for a moment, neither spoke.

"I'm sorry," they both blurted simultaneously, then laughed, breaking the tension.

"Ladies first," Mike said, setting down his pencil.

Abby stepped fully into the room. "No, you."

Mike ran a hand through his hair. "I'm sorry about how I left things this morning. I shouldn't have walked away from you like I did."

"And I shouldn't have pushed so hard," Abby replied, moving closer. "What are you doing up here, anyway?"

Mike glanced at his notepad, then back at her. "I wanted to see if I can blend your ideas with a few of my own for this room." He gestured to the sketches. "I thought maybe we could build a custom window seat that curves with the wall all the way around under the windows, complete with custom storage underneath. And then..." He looked above them toward the ceiling. "I was thinking skylights, four or five of them up there."

Abby moved to stand beside him, studying the detailed drawings in his notebook. He'd sketched built-in bookshelves along the interior walls, a window seat with storage underneath completely around the rest of the room, and a ceiling design that included large skylights.

"You did all this… for me?"

"I know how much this room means to you." Mike set his measuring tape down on the table. "I wanted to show you what it could be."

The simple sincerity in his voice made her heart ache.

"Mike…"

He took her hand then, his calloused palm warm against hers. "Abby, I need to say something, and I'd appreciate it if you'd just let me get it all out."

She nodded, suddenly unable to speak past the lump in her throat.

"I've been afraid," he began, his hazel eyes steady on hers. "Afraid of what starting something with you might mean for Tyler, afraid of what would happen when you went back to Charleston, afraid of opening myself up again after Cora died." His thumb traced small circles on the back of her hand. "But I realize now that I'm more afraid of letting you walk away without telling you how I feel."

Abby's heart hammered in her chest. "And how do you feel?"

"Like I've been waiting for you without even knowing it." The words came out strong and sure. "I know we haven't known each other long, not really. But there's something here, Abby, something real. I feel it every time we're together. And I think you feel it too."

"I do," she said, squeezing his hand. "That's actually what I came to tell you."

Mike's expression brightened.

"I'm not staying here for good."

"What about Charleston?" His voice was careful, measured.

"No. I'm not going back. I'm staying here."

"Really?"

"Yep. I'm staying in Laurel Ridge. I'm keeping the house."

A smile spread across his face, transforming his features. "And what about us?"

"That depends." Abby took a step closer. "What exactly are you offering?"

Mike chuckled, the sound warm and rich. "Direct as always. That's one of the things I love about you."

The word 'love' hung in the air between them.

"I want this to work, Abby. I want us to have a real chance." Mike's free hand came up to gently touch her cheek. "I know there will be complications. I come with a son who's lost a mother he never knew. My business is here, rooted in this community. But I believe you're the missing piece I didn't know I was looking for."

Mike's gaze was unwavering. "Tyler adores you, Abby. And I trust you. I trust that whatever happens between us, you'd never intentionally hurt him."

"I wouldn't," she affirmed.

"We'd take it slow with him, make sure he understands." Mike's voice grew thoughtful. "But kids are resilient, and often more perceptive than we give them credit for. I think he already senses there's something special between us."

"There is something special," Abby agreed.

"I feel the same way."

"So where do we go from here?" Abby asked.

"Forward," Mike said simply. "Together. One day at a time." He glanced at his sketches. "Starting with making this turret room everything you dream it could be. A space of your own."

Abby couldn't help the smile that spread across her face. "I think that sounds perfect, but let's hold off on any work here in this room."

He tilted his head, "But I thought..."

"Changed my mind. There's this special little boy who gave me a way better idea, and I think it suits this room much better."

Mike grinned, "A star gazing room."

"Yep. We have three floors in this house to work with. I think I'm going to create an office and a small showroom on the first floor. The second floor will be living space. The third floor... well... I don't even want to deal with this whole floor right away. But I know I want this room to be a star gazing room. The attic will be a personal retreat space, somewhere to go and shut out the world and just relax and enjoy life. Just be."

"I might know someone who could help you with all that," he said. "But seriously, Abby, I want you to stay here in Laurel Ridge because it's what you want. I only want you to be happy."

"It is what I want," she assured him. "This feels right. I'm home, Mike. This is where I want to be, and I want you and Tyler, if you'll have me."

Mike's smile was radiant. "I think that could be arranged."

He drew her closer, one hand still holding hers, the other moving to her waist. The touch was gentle but sure, giving her every opportunity to pull away if she wanted to.

She didn't.

Instead, Abby stepped into his embrace, tilting her face up to his. "I've never been good at the vulnerability thing," she admitted softly.

"You're doing just fine," Mike murmured, his gaze dropping to her lips.

"I'm scared," she whispered. "Terrified, actually. But in a good way."

"Me too." His voice was a low rumble that she could feel in her chest. "Worth it, though."

"Definitely worth it," she agreed.

And then Mike was kissing her, and everything else fell away. His lips were warm and gentle against hers. Abby's arms wound around his neck as she melted into him, feeling as though something long out of alignment had finally clicked into place.

When they eventually pulled apart, Mike rested his forehead against hers. "I've wanted to do that for a very long time."

"Since high school?" Abby teased.

Mike laughed, the sound reverberating through his chest. "My crush on you existed long before high school. Then took a little break when life took us in different directions. Then came back full circle the day you walked into my office."

"I was a goner the moment I saw you," Abby confessed, her fingers lightly tracing the line of his jaw. "Even if I didn't want to admit it."

Mike caught her hand and pressed a kiss to her palm. "Better late than never."

A shout from downstairs broke the moment. "Boss? You still up there? Need your input on this wiring!"

Mike rolled his eyes, but smiled. "Duty calls."

"Go," Abby said, reluctantly stepping back. "We have time."

"We do," he agreed, squeezing her hand once more before releasing it. "Dinner tonight? My place? Tyler's been begging to show you his science project."

"I'd love that."

Mike paused at the doorway, turning back to look at her standing in the center of the turret room, sunlight playing across her face. "You know what? Frank can wait another minute."

He crossed the room in three strides and pulled her into another kiss, this one deeper.

"Now I can go," he said with a grin, and disappeared out the door.

Abby hugged herself, feeling happiness so complete it was almost overwhelming. She walked to the window and gazed out at Laurel Ridge, the town that had always been her home, even when she'd tried to convince herself otherwise.

Her phone buzzed in her pocket.

A text from Leslie: *Well??*

Abby smiled and typed back: *I'm home for good.*

Three dancing emoji appeared instantly, followed by: *Dinner. Tomorrow. You're telling me EVERYTHING.*

Laughter bubbled up from deep within her. This was what it felt like to belong somewhere, to be surrounded by people who knew you and loved you anyway. This was what it felt like to come home.

"Thank you," she whispered to God, who had guided her journey even when she hadn't recognized His hand in it. "Thank you for bringing me home."

The future stretched before her, no longer a source of anxiety but of joyful anticipation. There would be more renovations, a business to build, a relationship to nurture, and perhaps someday, a family to expand. But for today, it was enough to simply be here, present in this moment, grateful for the unexpected journey that had led her exactly where she needed to be.

Abby Marshall had found her place. She was home.